PUSHKI...

The Minute Minders

'A book with heart and humour and a
bit of jeopardy, served up with a
light touch and a wink'
A.F. HARROLD

'Captivating . . . A treat for all ages'
PATRICIA FORDE
Laureate na nÓg and award-winning
author of *The Wordsmith*

'A funny, sweet fantasy adventure'
SARAH WEBB

'A fresh take on the "tiny person" theme
with a beautiful empathetic message!'
HARRIET MUNCASTER
author of the *Isadora Moon* series

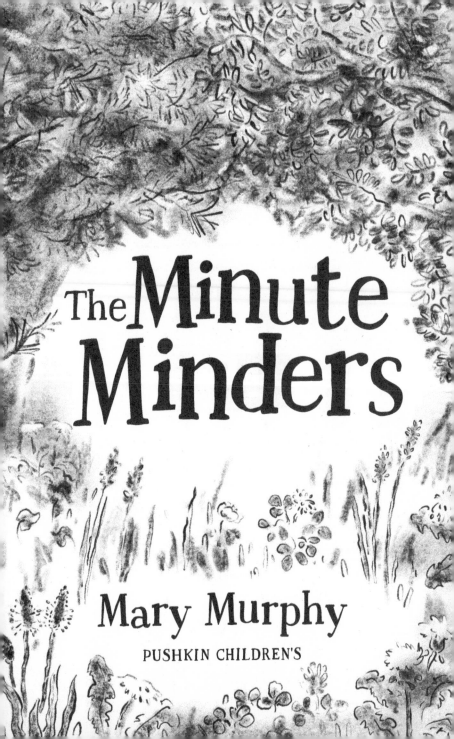

The Minute Minders

Mary Murphy

PUSHKIN CHILDREN'S

Pushkin Press

Somerset House, Strand

London WC2R 1LA

Text and illustrations © Mary Murphy, 2024

Minute Minders was first published by Pushkin Press in London, 2024

1 3 5 7 9 8 6 4 2

ISBN 13: 978-1-78269-422-9

The author received financial support from the Arts Council in the creation of this work

Designed and typeset by Jet Purdie

Printed and bound in the United Kingdom by Clays Ltd, Elcograf S.p.A.

www.pushkinpress.com

To my friend,

Patsy

Chapter 1

I remember seeing my first human like it happened just yesterday. I was seven years old, and it was a pretty big deal.

First, Dad made waffles with maple syrup for breakfast. We ate outside our cabin in the sunshine, and he gave me his 'get ready to see a human' talk again.

'Remember humans can't see us, or hurt us,' he said.

'I know,' I said.

'Even if they stamp on you, it's like a breeze...'

'Going through leaves,' I said.

'Don't be nervous,' Dad said.

'I'm not,' I said. More like terrified. 'Humans are just like us, right?'

'Well, they look like us,' Dad said carefully, 'if they're far away.'

'They're bigger,' I said.

'They *are* bigger,' Dad said. 'But that's not what's interesting about them. You know that humans don't even know we're working for them, because...'

'They can't see us,' I said. 'How big are they?'

'And you know 75% of fidders work for humans?'

'Yep. Big as a door? Big as a truck?'

'The thing is,' Dad said, 'being big doesn't mean you're scary. Like...' he looked around. 'That tree is not scary, right?'

I looked at the tree, reaching out of sight to the sky.

'A human is as big as a *tree?*' I said.

'No, no,' Dad said. 'A human would think that tree was big too.'

'So, are they as big as our cabin?' I said.

'I never measured a human,' Dad said, and took a huge bite of waffle. He had said all he was going to say.

Me and Dad lived together in a cabin outside Linbradan. This human we were going to see lived right in Linbradan, so we would travel by locator.

An adult human can walk four miles in an hour, but it would take a fidder days. We use locators to travel long distances. Locators look quite like the mobile phones that humans use, with silver buttons and a little screen. You type in where you want to go, press the 'locate' button, and *whirr* FIZZ... there you are, located. My dad had his own locator, given to him by his department. They relied on him to be in the right place at the right time, and he never let them down.

Now Dad took his locator out of his pocket, and keyed in the human's location.

'Will we be right beside the human?' I said.

'About five metres away,' Dad said. 'A two-minute walk. Okay?'

I nodded. I was nervous. Here I was, going to see a human, and what's more, travelling by locator. Locators almost always work, but you have to be careful with them.

I clamped my hand onto Dad's and he pressed the locate button.

It's hard to describe how locating feels. Your skin tingles like you're standing in a sparkling shower, and you get this thrilling, whirring feeling. The whirring gets faster, and you feel tickly, like there's a sparkler fizzing inside you. Then you open your eyes, and you've located.

I felt that *whirr* FIZZ now, and when it stopped I opened my eyes. Me and Dad were in a vast plain of waving green grass. Dad lifted me up, so I could see over the top of the grass. A few metres away was a blanket the size of our garden, and on the blanket lay the human.

I could see why folks said humans looked like fidders. This one had two legs and two arms, and one head with ears at the side and eyes at the front and so on. But it was pasty, and bald, and had no teeth, and kind of wobbled on its back, like an upturned beetle.

And it was big as a truck.

'Are they all this pale?' I asked.

'Nah, they got lots of colours, same as us,' Dad said. 'Come on, let's go closer.' He put me down, and I held his hand and hiked after him until we reached the edge of the giant blanket.

'Wait here, Stevie. I'm going right up,' Dad said. He clambered onto the thick blanket and made his way over its rumpled waves. I stayed put. Dad reached the giant human, and next thing, he leapt right onto the creature's hill of a belly.

'Be careful, Dad!' I yelled.

'It's asleep,' he shouted back.

Then the human's eyes opened, and it trembled like an earthquake. Dad jumped onto one arm, just as the other arm lifted like a great tree bough trying to snag a wisp of cloud from the sky. The raised arm dropped, and Dad toppled into the path of the falling hand.

'DAD!' I yelled — too late. The hand collapsed right on top of him, like a chest of drawers landing from space.

But... there was Dad. He made a 'ta-da!' movement with his arms. The human's eyes flicked towards him, then looked back to a twirl of cloud in the summer sky. Dad huffed and puffed his way back to me.

'See?' he said. 'They can't hurt you! No human can!'

'Except they could give me a heart attack,' I said.

'Aw, Stevie, did I scare you? I'm so used to humans, I forget what it's like, seeing them the first time.'

We watched

the human for a bit. It wiggled and wibbled and roared like a jungle bird.

When my breath had steadied, we located home, and Dad started washing fruit. Preparing excellent food was, in my opinion, Dad's most outstanding hobby.

'Let's have us some mambo smoothies,' he said.

'You mean mango?' I said. Ever since I was little, Dad sometimes mixed words up. 'Yes, please.'

Dad hummed and chopped fruit. 'So,' he said. 'Your first human.' He took out the blender. 'Will I put in banana?'

'I wonder what they think of us,' I said.

'But they don't know we exist,' Dad said. 'They can't see us. I'll put in banana.'

'I thought that human saw you,' I said. 'Just for a second.'

'You know what, Stevie,' Dad said. 'I've thought that too.' He sounded pleased. 'Sometimes I think the baby ones can see us.' He pressed the blender button and it started to roar. 'How about I put a peach in?'

he yelled.

I didn't answer.

Dad shared the smoothie mix into two glasses. When he offered me mine, he saw my face, and his eyebrows popped high. 'You okay, Stevie?'

'That human?' I said. I can still hear my voice wobbling. 'That was a *baby*?'

Dad put the smoothies on the worktop and crouched down to look me straight in the eye.

'Yes, that was a baby,' he said. 'I know humans seem very big, Stevie, but you'll get used to them. I promise. You'll even get to like them.'

'I won't,' I said. 'I'm going to steer clear of them. They scare me.'

'Some things you do, even if you're scared,' Dad said.

Chapter 2

Before I go on, let me explain some things.

My name is Stevie. Stevie Clipper. I'm a fidder, and I guess you're a human, right? So, the first thing I have to explain is what a fidder is.

You would say we fidders are tiny, if you could see us, and we say you humans are huge, because you are.

Our homes look like your homes, pretty much — we're not like mice, living in a hole in the wall, or sparrows in a nest. We have schools and hospitals and shops, and we grow our own fidder-sized vegetables.

Think of our homes like doll's houses maybe, but with stoves that heat, and toilets that flush, and lights that switch on and off.

Fidders live all around you. There are probably some living in your own home. We're not invisible, but we are invisible to humans. We see you though. Not all the time – that would be exhausting. We can kind of switch out of noticing you. Think of it like a hologram, one of those three-dimensional pictures that look like you could walk right into them. Fidders tilt the hologram one way, and see humans. We tilt it the other way, and see fidders. If we don't tilt the hologram, we don't see the humans.

'But Stevie,' I hear you say, 'when you met that baby human, you saw it *and* your dad. Neither of them disappeared, like in a hologram.'

That's true, human child.

'And also, there's a moment with a hologram

where you don't see either picture properly, you see a bit of both. We humans should be able to see fidders a bit!'

You're smart. Okay. It's not exactly like a hologram, but you get the idea.

Some fidders run fidder shops or restaurants, and we have our own teachers, doctors, police, radio announcers – all the people who make up a community. But nowadays most fidders work with humans. Dogs and cats too, although cats don't usually need our help.

Fidders have different departments for different kinds of human situations. And, just like humans, different individual fidders suit different kinds of work.

The Listeners Department employs quiet, focussed fidders.

Listeners flit around the human world, and when they feel an 'unhappy human' vibration they find that human, and listen to their thoughts, and feel their feelings. Then they refer the case to another department – like Dad's department, the Truth Revealers.

A Truth Revealer reveals the truth to a human, or between humans, especially when one of them is wrongly accused. Really important work, as Dad often said. When I grew up, I wanted to be a Truth Revealer just like him.

The Art Department matches ideas for stories, paintings or songs with a human artist.

The Luck Department tries to give a human a break if they've been having a run of bad luck.

The Pet Placement Agency matches a human with a pet, usually a dog or cat. Some lucky humans are matched with two pets, or even more.

The Sleeper Department mainly works with humans who have new babies, helping them sleep, or just giving them a daydreaming moment. Sleep Operators don't work with dogs or cats. Dogs and cats have sleep down to a fine art, from dozing, to napping, to all-night-through slumbering.

Then there's the Minute Minder Department. All the other departments regularly need Minute Minder help, so we're polite to Minute Minders, even though they drive us bonkers. More about Minute Minders later. They'll drive you bonkers too, guaranteed.

Only trained fidders are allowed talk to humans.

 See, an untrained fidder might accidentally let slip to humans that we fidders exist.

That's a big 'No way, José'.

'Why's that, Stevie?'

Good question, human child.

Well, if humans believed in us, they'd begin to imagine what we looked like. Humans are always imagining things. They'd think we were fairies, or leprechauns, or something. Would humans take advice from fairies? No. So we wouldn't be able to help humans any more.

'Then how come, Stevie Clipper, you are telling us about fidders, here in this very book?'

I thought you might ask that.

This book breaks the 'Don't tell humans about fidders' rule, it's true. But how many humans really believe what they read in a book like this? A book for kids?

This is a story I want to tell, but I just know you won't believe it.

Chapter 3

That time when I saw my first human, it was because I'd just turned seven and would be starting in Linbradan School soon. Then I'd see humans around town, so I had to know what to expect. City fidders grow up seeing humans everywhere, but our cabin was five miles from Linbradan, in the countryside, so I never saw humans when I was little.

Sure enough, I saw more humans when I started school. They were vast, and their voices were like thunder. When they moved past they cast shadows like storm clouds rolling in front of the sun, and the wind they made messed my hair. But Dad was right, I did get used to them, and I stopped being scared.

I also made friends with other fidder kids when I started school, which was pretty brilliant. If you've been alone a lot, you'll know how good it is to have even one friend. Humans and fidders, we're alike that way.

At school I learned stuff like Maths, Human Behaviour and Computer Skills. By the time I was nine I was on the basketball team, and my favourite subject was Art.

Outside of school it was just me and Dad in our cosy cabin, in the green light of the trees. Sometimes Dad's friends, the Larkins, visited. They ran Larkin Cab Service so they actually had their own Locator Cab. They brought pie, and we played cards, or Mrs Larkin played the accordion and taught us songs, and there was a lot of laughing. In summer the Larkin boys, Joe and Rory, were home from boarding school,

and we all rowed on the river near our cabin, like Dad
and Mr Larkin had done ever since they were little.

Mrs Larkin said our cabin was the best place in the
world. She wasn't wrong.

When I turned ten my classmates started

preparing to go to boarding school miles and miles north of Linbradan. That's what fidder kids from Linbradan usually did. All my school friends were going, but I didn't want to. I couldn't bear the idea of living apart from Dad. We're close.

See, long ago, a time I can't even remember, there was my mother, and my big brother Dicey, and my twin sister Annie, as well as me and Dad, all in the cabin together. Then one day when I was still a baby my mother went to Linbradan by locator with Dicey and Annie. Something went wrong, and they vanished.

Fidders hardly ever vanish on locator, and the ones who do, usually they come back in a few days. Mayor Hinchy came back, and he said it was like he was dreaming, nice dreams, all the time he was vanished. Sometimes I imagined my mother and Dicey and Annie, kind of floating and smiling on a soft duvet of cloud. I didn't worry about them. I didn't even remember them. I guess, though, some part of me missed them.

But I still had Dad, and he was all I needed. We were a team. I wanted to stay with him, and I figured out a solution. He could bring me to work, and school me there. I wouldn't have to leave Linbradan, or Dad.

Some fidders bring their kids to work. Fidder kids just sit quietly, poring over their books, while their parents work. When the adult fidder locates on assignment their kid goes too, bringing books with them to study all the while. Really. Almost all fidder kids are that well-behaved.

It took some persuasion to convince Dad. He thought I'd be bored going on assignment with him every day. Still, finally he said that if his boss agreed, we'd do it, and he smiled for the first time in hours.

He didn't want me to leave him either.

He phoned his boss,

Dee Hepburn, from our hall. (Fidders don't have mobile phones. You've seen old movies with humans using a phone that sits on a table in the hallway, or is fixed on the wall of a booth? That's what we have.)

Dad asked Dee if I could go to work with him. He told her I was never any trouble. He said I practically had superfidder powers of concentration. He kept his back to me on the call: he hated to look someone in the face when he lied.

Finally he said, 'Okay, Dee, thanks.' He hung up the receiver and turned to me, grinning. 'Dee says we can give it a try, starting tomorrow.' I whooped, and we hugged. My Dad always worked things out.

Chapter 4

First thing next morning, Dee Hepburn called us into her office before we even started work.

'I know you, Stevie,' Dee said. 'You're like your dad. You both like to help, you both have lots of ideas. But Stevie, you're not allowed to help here. No matter what. You have to stay on the sidelines and do exactly what your dad says. That's the only way this is going to work. Deal?'

'Deal,' me and Dad said. I already knew I wasn't allowed to get involved with humans, and I couldn't imagine wanting to.

My life as Dad's helper started well. He didn't see me as his helper. Dee didn't see me as his helper either. They thought I was just a kid, doing my schoolwork.

I didn't interfere with Dad's assignments. No sir. While Dad was working, I sat quietly and studied my books. But I also made our lunch sandwiches, and checked that Dad remembered his keys, and recharged his locator. I was a model helper, if I say so myself.

As time went on, I listened to what Dad said to his humans. After all, I wanted to be a Truth Revealer too, and this was my chance to learn from the master.

Dad was proud of how well I adapted to going to work with him. I was proud of how brilliant he was at Truth Revealing. That's how it was, for about a month.

The first time things were different was one sunny lunchtime in the park. Me and Dad sat high up on the back of a human's park bench, munching sandwiches and watching park life unfold.

Out of nowhere, a human boy came yelling and galumphing at us. A dog was chasing him. The human leapt onto our bench, rocking it so that we had to grab ourselves steady.

'We should tell him the dog is friendly,' I said to Dad. 'It's only a puppy.'

'It's not my case,' Dad said. He closed his eyes against the spring sunshine. 'I can't get involved unless it's my case.'

I knew quite a bit about working with humans

by now, and this boy needed help. I hopped onto his shoulder and said, 'Don't worry, the puppy just wants to be friends with you.'

Like all fidders, I could hear a human's thoughts. However, since I hadn't yet studied how to communicate with humans, I couldn't make them understand me. To this human boy, I sounded like a radio not properly tuned in, all crackles and buzz. (Yes! I could hear myself in his head, the way he heard me.)

Dad landed beside me on the boy's shoulder.

'Okay,' he said. 'Calm down.'

'I am calm,' I said.

'Not you. I'll talk to you later.'

'Oh.'

'This little dog just wants to play,' Dad said to the human. 'You stop yelling, he'll stop yipping.'

The boy stopped.

'Look at those puppy eyes,' Dad said.

The boy looked.

A human girl ran over. 'Come here, Tiny!' she bellowed. Tiny waggled, and the girl clipped on his lead.

'He's cute,' the boy roared. He climbed off the bench. 'Hi there, Tiny.' They both looked at Tiny like he was the eighth wonder of the natural world. They yelled some more and clomped away together. I could see they would be friends, even for just a few minutes.

'You can't butt in like that, Stevie,' Dad said. 'When that kid heard you buzzing at him, I had to fix things, but it wasn't my case. Plus, you're too young to talk to humans. Plus, you're not trained. Sheesh.'

'So train me,' I said. 'I'm ready. I've seen how you work.'

'It's not just about learning techniques,' Dad said. 'It's also about being older, and wiser, and less impulsive.'

'Like you?'

'Exactly.'

We watched the two humans ramble out of sight.

'Oh, well,' Dad said. 'Maybe we got away with it. Maybe nobody saw.'

But somebody always sees.

Chapter 5

Back at headquarters, Dee Hepburn called Dad to her office. When we arrived she looked up from her computer, folded her arms, and glared at Dad.

'You talked to that human who was scared of the dog,' she said. 'What were you thinking? That wasn't your assignment! It wasn't anyone's assignment!'

I started to say that I made Dad do it, but Dad dropped a 'be quiet' hand on my shoulder, and Dee raised a 'be quiet' hand too.

Dee said a Minute Minder saw what happened and complained. The complaint was that Dad had worked with a kid's fears. That wasn't a Truth Revealer's job – it was a Minute Minder's. They were cross as heck.

'I heard you actually started this, Stevie,' Dee said to me. 'You better watch your step.'

'The Minute Minders should be glad we helped,' I said. Out loud, unfortunately.

Dee gazed at me. Fidders can see human thoughts, but not each other's. Still, I had a pretty good idea what Dee was thinking, and it wasn't complimentary.

'Hal,' Dee said. 'If Stevie is coming to work with you, she has to understand about Minute Minders, and she has to know to keep out of human business, one hundred percent. Convince her. By tomorrow.'

So, that evening, Dad set about convincing me. First, he explained about Minute Minders.

When a particularly tricky case crops up, Dad said, and another fidder department can't solve the problem, they ask the Minute Minder Department

29

for help. All the other departments rely on Minute Minders at one time or another.

Sounds important, I thought.

A Pet Placement Agent can only work with a pet situation. An Arts Executive can only work with an artist. A Luck Department Official can only work with someone who is having a run of bad luck. But Minute Minders can intervene anywhere, with anyone.

For example, if a Pet Placement Agent places a dog with a human, and things don't go smoothly, they can ask a Minute Minder to help. The Minute Minder might talk to the human about helping the dog change a habit. More likely they'll talk to the dog, because dogs can change more easily than humans.

Sounds interesting, I thought.

Minute Minders have huge files that give them privileged information on the human's family, history and dreams.

Also interesting, I thought.

Unlike other fidders,

a Minute Minder has just one minute per assignment per day. One precious minute for one mixed-up human.

Why do Minute Minders have only one minute?

First of all, Minute Minders work with a human's thoughts or feelings. It's not good to interfere too much with a human's thoughts or feelings. The humans have to make up their own minds. You probably won't over-influence your human in just a minute.

Second, Minute Minders like to introduce ideas slowly and carefully to their human. One minute per day feels about right.

Third, every Minute Minder Department in the world is too short-staffed to give time willy-nilly. They have to spread themselves thin. A minute a day is all they can give to a case.

Sounds easy, I thought.

Finally, the Minute Minder Department would collapse under paperwork if they spent more than a minute per day on a case, because Minute Minders do mountains of research, and write countless reports, files, memos and feedback forms.

Sounds boring, I thought.

'Mrs Larkin used to be a Minute Minder,' Dad said. 'But she said it was too strict. There were too many rules and revelations, and endless paperwork.'

'Rules and revelations?'

'Rules and regulations, I mean.' He shook his head. 'Mrs Larkin had to cancel vacations, just to catch up on paperwork. And she had practically a whole library of rules to learn. Minute Minders have plenty of rules. Way too plenty, in my humble opinion.'

Sounds depressing, I thought.

'Not my cup of tea,' Dad said. 'I like things

more relaxed.'

'Me too,' I said.

'So that's the deal with Minute Minders,' Dad said. 'We have to respect them, and not tread on their toes.'

'Sure,' I said. 'No more interfering. A Minute Minder might see.'

'Just do your schoolwork and let me get on with my work, or you'll be sent to boarding school.'

Okay, I definitely didn't want that to happen.

I would have to go against all my instincts and impulses not to help humans – and not to help Dad, even when he needed it.

Chapter 6

Working with Dad was interesting, although I missed my friends who were all now far away in boarding school. I guess most kids want to be with other kids, at least some of the time. So I liked it best when Dad worked with human kids. He liked working with kids best too. Kids and dogs.

CASE HC43D/Blink-Paudie

One of the first kids Dad was assigned to was Paudie Blink. Paudie was from Tassimity, a big city way north of Linbradan, and he was spending this half term with his Granny Blink in Linbradan.

At first, Paudie and his Granny had a fine time. They played dominoes, hiked in the hills, and talked to Poe, Granny's pet crow. And they inspected Granny Blink's treasure.

The treasure was upstairs, on the chest of drawers, in a wooden box with a silver kangaroo on the lid.

The box held Granny's cameo earrings, a silver bracelet with charms, and, in a small paper envelope, a curl of her baby hair that Paudie didn't like to touch.

The kangaroo box also held mementoes of Grandad Blink. There were his silver cufflinks, his wedding ring, a medal he won in a relay race, and his gold tie-pin with a real emerald.

This tie-pin was Paudie's favourite treasure. He liked to hold it up to Granny Blink's bedroom window and watch the light play through the green emerald.

Then one day Granny Blink said, 'Paudie, pet, did you borrow Grandad's tie-pin?'

'No, Granny.'

'Well, *someone* took it.'

They searched everywhere, but didn't find the tie-pin. Granny Blink suspected that Paudie had taken it for himself, and Paudie knew she suspected him.

Then the cufflinks disappeared.

Then Granny Blink's charm bracelet.

Luckily, Harry Cruise from the Listeners Department passed by, and picked up the 'unhappy human' vibration.

He listened to Paudie's thoughts. He listened to Granny Blink's thoughts. He sat by the kangaroo box, and watched.

At last Harry saw Poe lift the lid of the box with

his strong beak, drag a shining silver chain from it, and poke the chain through a little gap between two floorboards on the landing.

Harry located to headquarters, and asked Dee Hepburn to assign a Truth Revealer to reveal that Poe, not Paudie, was the criminal. Paudie was taking the train home to Tassimity later today, so there wasn't much time. Dee gave the assignment to her best operator – Dad.

Me and Dad located straightaway to the Blink home, where Paudie and Granny were hustling into the car to bring Paudie to the train station.

'Have you your pocket money, Paudie?'

Paudie fished some coins from his pocket to show Granny, but one coin fell glinting to the ground. Poe swooped down and swept it up.

'Poe, you thief!' I said. But I didn't have the locator translator.

The locator translator allows even untrained fidders to talk to animals. It works for French, Chinese, Dog, Fish, Raccoon and so on. It's hard luck that humans don't have translators to talk with their own dogs and cats.

'You're in big trouble, Poe!' I said.

'Hush, Stevie,' Dad said. Then he spoke into

Granny Blink's ear. 'Maybe *Poe* is the culprit.'

'Jeepers, that never crossed my mind!' Granny thought. 'Poe!' she yelled. 'I have my suspicions of you, you blaggarding bird!'

Poe flapped away into the house.

'Follow him!' Dad said.

'Come on Paudie,' Granny said. 'Let's you and me

see what Poe is at.'

I hung on to Dad, and Dad hung on to Granny's shoulder, and she ran into the house and thumped up the stairs, followed by Paudie, just in time to see Poe pushing Paudie's coin between the floorboards.

'Poe, you bandit!' Granny said. 'Poe, you crook!' She fetched tools and eased a floorboard up, enough for Paudie to reach down and feel about. He found his coin, the key to the shed, some shining bottle caps, and all Granny Blink's lost treasure, including the emerald tie-pin.

Granny said sorry to Paudie for suspecting him. Paudie said it was okay.

'I bet he doesn't really feel it's okay,' I said.

'He does,' Dad said.

'How can you tell?'

'I just tuned in, and I sensed it.'

I tried to tune in.

'I can only hear his thoughts,' I said. 'I can't sense what he feels.'

'That's because you're not trained, Stevie,' Dad said. 'Hearing his thoughts is enough, at your age.'

Paudie was late for his train and had to stay another night with Granny, which was fine by him, and he missed his first day back at school, also fine by him.

'That was good,' I said.

'It was,' Dad said. 'But you shouldn't have talked to Poe.'

'I'm allowed talk to crows,' I said.

'You're not allowed talk to *anyone* I'm working with – crow, dog, cat, human.'

'Sorry, Dad,' I said.

Somebody saw, of course.
Somebody always sees.
And they reported us.

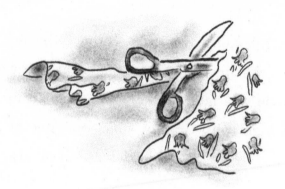

Chapter 7

A few days later, Dad had to reveal to Sandra May Bee that she couldn't have a new party dress. The Bee family did not have enough money right now. Luckily, Sandra May would look just dandy in her cousin's party dress.

CASE HC47C/Bee-Sandra May

'I'm going to copycat her mother,' Dad said.

The locator has a brilliant function called 'copycat'. You can input a recording of any voice, and the human will hear your words in that voice. It could be the human's own voice, or their mother or father or teacher, or a musician or hero they admire.

So Dad copycatted Sandra May's mother's voice into the locator, and we located to Sandra May's bedroom. I did some art while Dad worked. I drew Sandra May, with her dark curls and shining brown eyes. The dress I drew for her was all over bluebells, same fabric as her bedspread and curtains.

'Look at this, Dad,' I said, and showed him my picture.

'Wow,' Dad said. 'Her bedspread would make a spectacular dress.'

Fidders talk 'one-to-one' when they don't want the human to hear, but unfortunately Dad didn't do that this time. Sandra May heard him too, like she was hearing an idea of her own. Dad doesn't often make mistakes, but this was one.

'Oh yeah!' Sandra May thought back. 'I can easily make a dress! It'll be *fabulous*!'

'Wait, Sandra May!' Dad said. But it was too late.

Snip, snip.

Sandra May was one of those headstrong, grab-any-idea humans.

Snippity-snip.

When they make up their mind, you might as well retire right then.

The party dress did not turn out well.

'Sorry, Dad,' I said.

'Heck, I'm not sure which of us messed up that assignment,' Dad said.

'Oh well,' I said. 'Nobody saw.'

But somebody always sees.

They reported Dad.

I promised myself more than ever to act invisible when Dad was working. It was hard. If I saw a human in trouble, something came over me, and I found myself trying to help. Some fidders are built that way.

Mikey O'Grady was eight. He set up a stall outside his house to sell seaside pebbles he found on vacation. He made a sign that said: *Magic Pebbles 50c each.*

But Mikey's pebbles were not magic. Dad's assignment was to have Mikey make a truthful sign.

We located to Mikey's shoulder. He was at his stall, his pebbles set out in rows. I floated down and strolled between the different-coloured pebbles – ochre, pink, mauve, green, terracotta. And the patterns – striped, spotty, patchy, chipped with glitter.

'They sure look magic,' I called to Dad.

'But they're not,' Dad called back. I drifted back up to him, and he started whispering to Mikey.

45

'Mikey,' Dad said. 'You know it isn't true the pebbles are magic.'

'They are,' Mikey thought back.

'What makes them magic?' I asked Dad.

'Be quiet, Stevie.'

'Just ask him! He must have an idea why they're magic. Just ask him, Dad, I mean if they're magic then—'

'Okay, okay!' Dad said. He spoke into Mikey's head. 'Mikey, what makes your pebbles magic?'

Mikey reflected.

'They make you happy,' he thought back. 'That's the magic.'

'Good answer,' I said. 'What's more magic than making someone happy? Admit it Dad, the pebbles *are* magic!'

'Let me do my job, Stevie,' Dad said, and I hushed up.

A woman stopped and read Mikey's sign.

'Magic pebbles, Mikey?' she said. She picked one up: sage green, with a belt of pink. 'Really?'

'Look at it properly, Mrs Deegan,' Mikey said. 'Doesn't it make you happy? That's the magic.'

Mrs Deegan looked.

Bit by bit she remembered, for the first time in many years, her own childhood vacations by the sea. She remembered the taste of the warm, salty air. She remembered yelling gulls and tickly waves, and she remembered collecting pebbles.

'You know what, Mikey?' she said. 'It does make me happy.' She gave Mikey 50c.

'See?' I said. 'They *are* magic! The sign is truthful.'

'I think you're right,' Dad said. 'But Stevie, you distracted me.'

'Sorry,' I said. 'But I only spoke to you. I'm allowed to do that.'

As usual, somebody saw, and they reported us to

Dee. Dee called us to her office.

She said she knew
Mikey believed the sign
told the truth, so she
agreed he could keep it.

But she had more to say.

'Stevie really seems to mess things up, Hal. She talks to a human, she talks to a crow, she talks to you. Even that time when she drew a picture of a party dress, it made trouble.' Dee looked at me. 'You're on your last chance, Stevie. One more complaint and you can pack your bags for boarding school.'

Boarding school. No cabin, no trees, no fields of summer barley. No Dad.

'And Hal, one more complaint and you lose your job.'

Face it, I said to myself. The
complaints are usually my fault.
I have to butt out of Dad's
work one hundred percent.

I could do that. Right?

Chapter 8

A couple of weeks later, Dad had another assignment with Sandra May Bee, the kid who chopped up her bedspread.

CASE HC47C/Bee-Sandra May

We browsed Sandra May's new file. One look at her photo and you were ready to swear in a court of law that she was kind to animals, and probably sang to flowers. But boy, was she headstrong. She'd do something rash, then get panicky as a chicken, and clam up.

Yesterday's example: she scribbled

Mister Prisby is preposterous

on the board. Mr Prisby asked, 'Who wrote this?' Sandra May's mind went *dah-de-dah* like he wasn't even talking, and she said nothing.

Today's example: she painted wings on Paul Scully's dolphin drawing. 'It'll look *amazing*!' she thought. It didn't. She panicked and slid the drawing behind the bookshelves.

'Has anyone seen Paul's drawing?' Mr Prisby said. *Dah-de-dah.*

'She's just impetuous,' Dad said. 'We'll help her tell the truth.'

'The Luck Department are in charge,' I said. 'See? Page four.' Sometimes Dad just skimmed a file.

Now he turned to page four and read it properly.

The Bee family were having bad luck, *Details*

Confidential.

Sophie Grass from the Luck Department was working with the family, and Dad had to liaise with her. All the Linbradan departments shared a canteen, and that's where we met Sophie Grass to discuss the case.

Should Sandra May be lucky, or should she be found out?

I stayed quiet, like Dad told me.

'I wish Sandra May could be lucky,' Sophie said.

'You Luck guys want everyone to be lucky,' Dad said. 'But not everyone can be lucky.'

'You think I don't know that?' Sophie Grass said.

'If one person gets lucky,' Dad went on, 'someone else gets unlucky.'

'I tell you, I know that! We study this stuff!'

My dad, sometimes he riles other folk.

A Sleeper Operator called Max was at the next table, drinking Bedtime Tea. He overheard us.

'Hey, how about I send them all to sleep for ten

minutes?' Max drawled. 'You can get the dolphin painting out from behind the shelves. Nobody gets in trouble.'

Now Dad was riled.

'Mind your own beeswax!' he said. 'Your department isn't even involved.'

'Sheesh, sorry I spoke.' Max yawned.

'Max's idea could work,' Sophie said.

'No way!' Dad said. 'It'll take a month to get the Sleeper Department involved.' (The folks in the Sleeper Department are snoozy, and slow to take action.)

'Maybe we need a round table,' Sophie said.

'Aw, no!' I said. Sometimes you can't stay completely quiet.

'Hush up, Stevie,' Dad said. 'But Sophie. We. Don't. Need. A. Round. Table.'

However, Sophie Grass went ahead and arranged a round table for that afternoon.

At a round table, the case is discussed and a negotiator suggests a way forward. Today, Sophie attended from the Luck Team, Max from the Sleeper Department (however he got involved all of a sudden), Dad from the Truth Revealers, with me in tow, and Dee Hepburn was the negotiator.

They talked and talked, but they couldn't agree on a plan. Then Dee said, 'How about we call in a Minute Minder?'

'Wonderful,' Sophie said.

'Cool,' Max said.

'No!' Dad said. 'Not cool! We can figure this out ourselves.'

Dad was overruled. Dee called in Minute Minder Andrea Bax. Andrea Bax said she'd be happy to help – in eight days' time. She didn't have a spare minute before then.

Dee asked Dad to stay on the case for those eight days. If he saw Sandra May making trouble again, he should record it for her file.

'You're on obbo,' Dee said to Dad. She turned to me. 'That means you too, Stevie.'

Back home, Dad was in a bad mood.

When Dad's in a bad mood, he cooks pasta.

Clatter the pan, chop chop *chop* the onion.

'Obbo!' He threw spinach into a strainer and shook it dizzy. 'OBBO!'

'What's obbo anyway?' I said.

'Short for observation. You watch what's going on, and get to know your human better. Obbo! That's for rookies.' He shook the spinach some more. 'Am I a rookie? No! I'm Hal Clipper, licensed professional.'

'Don't do anything reckless, Dad,' I said.

To be fair to him, Dad didn't do anything reckless. I did.

Next morning, me and Dad located to Sandra May's classroom window sill. Sandra May stood by the window. She wore a white dress, blue cardigan and silver sandals with little blue jewels on them. I had an attack of sandal-envy.

Mr Prisby arrived. 'Morning, all!' he said, and put his books and spectacles on his desk. Everyone went to sit down.

'Obbo,' I reminded Dad.

'I know, I know,' he said.

Walking to her own desk, Sandra May passed Mr Prisby's, and had one of her crazy impulses. She slipped his spectacles into her pocket.

'If Mr Prisby has no glasses,' she thought, *'we'll* have to read everything for him. We can make it all up! It'll be *brilliant!'*

'Like that'll happen,' I thought.

In a moment, Mr Prisby said, 'Has anyone seen my specs?' and glared around the classroom. It dawned on Sandra May that he might not see the funny side of things. *Dah-de-dah.* In a panic, she dropped the spectacles into the nearest schoolbag, which happened to belong to Zofia Kaminski.

So far, me and Dad, we were doing an excellent job of obbo.

But Sandra May's thoughts showed she would happily tell a big fat lie and get Zofia Kaminski in trouble.

I forgot about staying in Linbradan.

I forgot about Dad keeping his job.

I zipped up to Sandra May's shoulder and yelled, 'Don't be so *scaredy*, Sandra May! Don't be so *mean*! Tell the truth!'

Buzz, buzz, Sandra May heard.

'Not again, Stevie,' Dad groaned. 'What happened to obbo?' He glided up beside me, on Sandra May's shoulder.

You're probably wondering if fidders can fly. No, we can't. We're not fairies. When I say Dad glided here, or I zipped there, it's because we're so light, compared to humans, we can do these big leaps and kind of float around, catching air currents, maybe like little paper planes.

Not flying.

Not fairies.

Back to the story.

'Hey,' Dad said gently to Sandra May. 'Don't make trouble for Zofia. Tell Mr Prisby the truth. He'll understand.'

Sandra May paused. The mean part of her told her to let Zofia Kaminski take the blame.

But my dad had handled this right. Sandra May plucked the spectacles back out of Zofia's bag, held them up and said, 'I have them, Mr Prisby.' Everyone looked at her, and she went red.

'Thanks for owning up, Sandra May,' Mr Prisby said. 'We'll talk later.'

At breaktime, Sandra May told Mr Prisby about writing 'Mr Prisby is Preposterous' on the board, and drawing on Paul Scully's dolphin drawing, and where she hid it.

The truth was revealed. Dad said that was all he could do. He couldn't help it if humans kept getting themselves in trouble.

'Who knows?' he said. 'Maybe Sandra May will see that telling the truth can turn out right. Maybe it will help her be nicer. Humans are unpredictable.'

'Not likely,' I said. 'If it wasn't for you, she would have let Zofia get in trouble. She was thinking mean.'

'Well, we've done our best,' Dad said. 'Even if we messed up on obbo.' He didn't point out that it was me who had messed up. Again.

Of course somebody saw. Somebody always sees.

A Minute Minder called Chuck Beluga was working with Paul Scully, the dolphin artist. Paul was always drawing dolphins. Chuck's assignment was to persuade Paul to control the dolphin-drawing and do a little schoolwork.

Chuck's minute overlapped the time when Dad jumped on Sandra May's shoulder. He saw the whole darn thing.

Was he impressed? Maybe.

Was he angry? Boy, he sure was.

He reported Dad.

Chapter 9

Next morning, Dee called us to her office.

'Sandra May was a Minute Minder assignment, Hal,' Dee said, 'and they're furious. You already had your final warning. The way I see it, you have three options.' She lifted up a finger for every option. 'One: you go on special assignment. Two: I fire you. Or three: I take early retirement.'

'Right,' Dad said.

'And I'm not taking early retirement.'

'What's the special assignment option?' I said.

Dee pushed a thick yellow folder towards us.

'This,' she said. 'Sandra May Bee.'

Dad said, 'She's the one who got us into all this trouble.'

(Actually, I was the one who got us into all this trouble.)

Dee patted the folder. 'Read her family file. It's revealing.'

We read.

When Linbradan Candle Factory closed down last month, Sandra May Bee's parents lost their work, and soon they

would lose their home. Then their four kids would go live with different relatives, while the parents found new jobs and a new home to rent. Sandra May would go to live with an aunt in Tassimity. She didn't even know it yet.

'I want to send you to Tassimity, to help Sandra

May,' Dee said. 'She'll find it hard, leaving Linbradan.'

'Not Tassimity!' I said. 'We'd find it awful hard, too.'

'I know, Stevie,' Dee said. 'But this way, you stay with your dad. This way, he still has a job, and if you both do good in Tassimity, maybe you can come back to Linbradan.' She looked at Dad.

'I don't see we have a choice,' he said.

That evening, me and Dad talked.

'Can't you get another job in Linbradan?' I said.

'Not after all the complaints,' he said. 'A small-time agent like me.'

'But you're the best Truth Revealer in town!'

Dad patted my back.

'We could go to Mexico,' I said. 'I bet they need Truth Revealers there.'

Mexico.

That was where Dad and Mom had dreamed of going even before they were married. Now me and Dad dreamed of it. We often looked at maps of Mexico, and cooked Mexican food, and listened to Mexican music. It was like talking about Mom without saying her name.

Dad said, 'Tassimity isn't all bad.'

'I know plenty about Tassimity,' I said. 'It's noisy, and crowded. Everyone's out for themselves, and nobody makes friends.'

'You can make friends anywhere,' Dad said. 'And at least we'll still be together.'

I thought about Sandra May Bee, going all alone to Tassimity.

Yes. At least me and Dad, we'd still be together.

But we were losing our friends and the home we loved.

And it was all my fault.

Or was it *all* my fault? Part of me said it was Sandra May Bee's fault too.

I wished we had never met her.

The next week was a cyclone of packing and telephoning and saying goodbye. Sometimes, between packing boxes, I just lay on the ground under a buttercup, looking between the shining yellow petals to the sky, pretending we would never leave.

But you can't pretend reality away. Tassimity day came. Sunlight played through the leaves, and a blackbird sang his heart out in our tree, and I felt sadder every minute. Mr Larkin arrived at our cabin, to bring us to Tassimity by locator cab. (Dad had already returned his work locator to the Truth Revealers Department.)

Mr Larkin said, 'Everyone will miss you, Hal.'

'We'll miss everyone, too,' Dad said.

'Ready?'

'Ready.'

I took Dad's hand and pressed my eyes shut, partly because that's what I always do on locators, and partly to stop myself crying.

I felt the familiar wobbly *whirr* FIZZ ... and in a moment everything steadied again. Before I opened my eyes, I smelled diesel fumes, and fried food, and heard rackety-track trams, and the laughing and shouting of hundreds of humans. Then I opened my eyes. Looming buildings, honking cars, traffic lights, humans shouldering between each other – this was it. Tassimity.

Chapter 10

The Opportunity Providers had found an apartment for us right bang where Sandra May's aunt lived. Our apartment was high up, surrounded by sky. The balcony looked out over Beckett Park, and beyond that we saw the jam-packed city, and way far away the distant gleam of ocean.

Our new address was 92-D, Delvin Tower, Lennox Street, Beckett, Tassimity. Our apartment block was set in a front corner of a humans' block, also called Delvin Tower. Sandra May's aunt, Jane Bee, lived in 10-C. The human block was ten floors high, and the fidder block was one hundred floors. Ten fidder floors for every human floor.

Tassimity was loud and hard-edged, all curbs and glass and concrete, just like I expected. And the lights – streetlights, car lights, flashing signs, shop windows. They made me tired. Sad, stunted trees grew along some streets. The few birds living in them didn't even try to call over the griping, grinding traffic.

Beckett Park though, right across from our apartment, had full-grown trees, and a lake, and tribes of birds and squirrels. It wasn't Linbradan, but it was the best we had for now.

We arrived in Tassimity on a Friday, and spent the weekend unpacking. Our apartment was untidy from the beginning, just like our cabin in Linbradan. There were books and art things on the table, or photos from Linbradan, or maybe the parts of a clock or radio that Dad was planning to fix. Also, there were cooking things everywhere. Dad loved to cook, and he cooked like a pro – a pro with about seven assistants to clean up after him.

On Monday me and Dad had breakfast on our balcony, wrapped up against the cool morning air. Then we started making art. I tried to draw the swooping gulls, using charcoal. My page filled with twirling, crumbly lines. Dad was painting blobby clouds.

'When will you start work, Dad?' I asked.

'Dee said someone will contact me,' Dad said. He had blue paint in his hair.

'I wish there was a job where you could just do art,' I said.

'Or be an explorer,' Dad said. We listed some other great jobs: gardener, detective, sailor, roadie for a band.

Our doorbell rang, and I went with Dad to answer it. A birdlike fidder stood outside. Not like a cute garden bird, more like a grumpy parrot.

'Clipper?' she said. Her voice was harsh. 'And Stevie.' She glowered at me. 'I'm Trent.' She swept past us, banged my leg with her briefcase, yanked out a chair and sat down. We stared. She said, 'You got our memo?'

'No,' Dad said.

'Confound it. Well, I'm from the Minute Minder Department.' She plucked a file from her briefcase and handed it to Dad.

'Sandra May's file,' she said. 'Get to know it.'

'We already saw her files,' I said, 'Her party dress file, her school file, her family file.'

'This is her Tassimity file,' Miss Trent said, looking at me like I was a bad smell. She turned to Dad. 'You'll be working with Sandra May, Clipper, and it's a Minute Minder case, so you'll become a Minute Minder.'

'A Minute Minder?' Dad said shakily. 'Me? I don't think I'm Minute Minder material.'

'We're so short-staffed, we'll try anyone,' Miss

Trent said. 'No offence.' She started flicking through a spiral-bound notebook. 'You'll be a trainee, and you'll have a supervisor. Me.' She found the page she wanted. 'Now, I'll update you on Sandra May Bee.'

We listened, a bit dazed. The Minute Minders sure don't hang about.

'Sandra May still has some time left in Linbradan,' Miss Trent said.

'She'll love that,' Dad said.

Miss Trent ignored him.

'Then she'll live with her aunt, Jane Bee.' Miss Trent coughed. 'She's never met Jane Bee.'

'She'll hate that,' I said.

Miss Trent ignored me.

'You'll have about three months of training, Clipper, then you'll work with Sandra May.'

'Three months?' Dad said.

'What about me?' I said. 'Can I come to work with Dad, like in Linbradan?'

'Hmm.' Miss Trent flicked through her notes. 'Yes,

the Chief says you can be with your dad. And you have to keep a journal of lessons learned from your dad's assignments.'

'I have to?'

'Don't blame me,' she said. 'I don't make the rules.'

She gave Dad a trainee locator, barely powerful enough to let us pooter around Tassimity, never mind visit Linbradan. Then she said he should come in tomorrow to start his training, and said no thank you to a cup of tea, and left.

'Wow,' I said.

'Yeah,' Dad said.

'We're going to be Minute Minders,' I said.

'Actually, Stevie,' Dad said. 'Maybe you shouldn't come to work with me. You can't seem to help jumping in and complicating things.'

'I've learned my lesson,' I said. 'I promise. Just give me a chance, Dad.'

Dad could see I meant it.

And as usual he gave in.

He looked at his locator.

'Fancy exploring?' he said. 'We can go wherever we like.'

'Wherever we like in Tassimity, you mean,' I said.

And I had to admit Tassimity was plenty big for now. First, we went shopping, and Dad bought a new backpack for work, and I bought a notebook for the journal Miss Trent insisted I keep. On its cover I wrote VIPS (VITALLY IMPORTANT POINTS).

Then we wandered around the city. We basked in the colours and aromas of Little India, Little China, Little Italy and Little Mexico (our favourite, of course). We roamed around theatres and galleries, dazzling shops, and parks crammed with flowers and play areas. It was dizzying.

But it was no Linbradan.

Chapter 11

When we got home, there was a huge parcel waiting for us. Dad inspected it, careful and excited, like a dog checking out a beetle.

'It's from the Minute Minder Department,' he said.

Then he opened it.

Books! Brilliant!

But no.

These were not books you would want to read. These were study books, chock-a-block with rules, regulations and case histories.

This parcel could put anyone off parcels for life.

We put the books on shelves in Dad's bedroom: rulebooks on one shelf, technique books higher up. Dad said he didn't need to read them; he'd pick up the rules as he went along. But I started reading them right away. Maybe if I learned the rules, I could help Dad keep this job, and make up for losing the last one.

Next morning we located to outside Minute Minder Headquarters, a skyscraper built of steel, glass and dignity. There were some shabby alleys of diners and laundromats nearby, but the buildings on the main street looked brand spanking new.

We went up the steps, and the doors swished open for us. Inside was like a new planet, vast and silent. We approached the shining reception desk.

'Morning!' Dad said, and showed the receptionist a letter from Miss Trent.

The receptionist glanced at the letter, then darted

a cool look at me. 'There are two of you?' he said.

'Me and Dad, we're allowed stay together,' I said.

'Dad and I,' the receptionist said. His nametag said Francesco Rossi.

'Oh yeah,' I said. (In case you don't know, it's bad grammar to say 'me and Dad'.) 'Anyway, we're allowed.' Francesco Rossi didn't say, 'Like I could care less.' Not out loud.

'You want office 16-4, floor 16,' he said.

'Thanks, Frankie, pal,' Dad said. Francesco Rossi looked taken aback, then almost smiled, but changed his mind, or forgot, or didn't know how.

We walked to the lift, the carpet sucking all sound from our footsteps. Dad whistled to cheer things up. On the next floor, three more fidders sidled into the lift. Nobody spoke. Dad stopped whistling.

We edged out of the lift on floor 16 and found office 16-4. Miss Trent opened the door almost before Dad knocked on it, and ushered us in. Her office had a grey, ribbed carpet and white walls. A table near the window carried a small jungle of healthy plants. I couldn't imagine any plant daring to be sickly in Miss Trent's office. One wall was shelved with rulebooks and technique books, all perfectly organised and dust-free. The other walls displayed photographs of young fidderfolk; Miss Trent's trainees, she told us, all now effective Minute Minders in this very city. 'None of my trainees fail,' she said, pinning us with her sharp eyes.

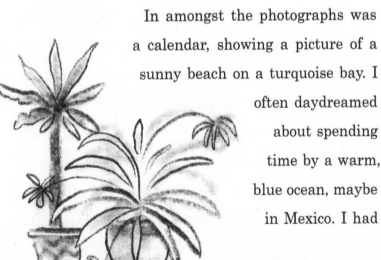

In amongst the photographs was a calendar, showing a picture of a sunny beach on a turquoise bay. I often daydreamed about spending time by a warm, blue ocean, maybe in Mexico. I had

never even
been to the
cold, grey
ocean of
Tassimity
Docklands.
How would
it be, on that calendar
beach, paddling, or
snorkelling, or sipping a pineapple
smoothie in a hammock?

'Sit down, you both,' Miss Trent said. We sat at one side of her desk, and she sat opposite us, and looked at Dad. 'You don't look happy, Clipper,' she said. 'Don't you *want* to be a Minute Minder?'

'I'd prefer to be a Truth Revealer,' Dad said.

'Not possible,' Miss Trent said. She drummed her fingers. 'You know there's an amazing bonus if you qualify as a Minute Minder?' Dad didn't look convinced. The bonus was probably a new rulebook or something.

'When you become a licensed Minute Minder...' Miss Trent paused like a game show host... 'you get three weeks with the Vacation Locator...' phantom drum roll... 'anywhere in the whole world!'

'No way!' me and Dad said together.

'Yes, way,' Miss Trent said.

'So you might want to try your best, Clipper.' I was on Miss Trent's side now. Anywhere in the world! Me and Dad looked at each other and mouthed the magic word: Mexico!

'Now,' Miss Trent said. 'I'll ask you some basic rules, Clipper. To see where you are.'

'Hit me,' Dad said.

'Rule 19, Section A.' She waited. 'You better know this,' her flinty eyes seemed to say.

Dad took a shot.

'Rule 19, Section A,' he said. '*A Minute Minder Must be on Time for his Human.*'

'That's Rule Number One.'

'Isn't Rule Number One *Do Right by Your Human?*' Dad said.

'That's Fidder Rule Number One.' Miss Trent's voice was arctic. 'And yes, it's our most important rule. But I'm asking you rules specific to Minute Minders.' I wiggled. I didn't like Miss Trent being sharp with

Dad. She looked at me.

'You know it, Stevie?' she asked.

'Rule 19, Section A,' I said. '*Every Minute Used Must be Filed Under a Specific Category*'.

'Precisely,' she said. 'Try another, Clipper.'

Dad didn't know any rule Miss Trent asked him. I knew them all. The rules weren't hard, there were just lots of them.

Next morning, Miss Trent gave Dad a written assessment, hoping he might do better on paper. He didn't.

'You don't even know Rule 4, Section B?' Miss Trent said, reading his answers. 'You, Stevie?'

'Rule 4, Section B: *Humans are Not Obliged to Take Advice from Minute Minders*.'

'Precisely.' For a moment she looked faintly pleased. Then she didn't. 'Stevie, how come you know the rules?'

'I just read some of Dad's books,' I said.

She turned to Dad. 'Remember, Clipper, some training books are unsuitable for children.'

'Oh, sure,' Dad said. 'Of course.' He waited for a hint, then asked, 'Which ones?'

'Well, anything about talking to humans,' Miss Trent said. Dad nodded. 'And the books about report-writing are too complex.' Like I would have read those anyway.

Miss Trent and Dad spent the afternoon going through some rules and case histories, while I did a little History, a little Human Knowledge, and wrote a poem about the beach in the calendar. It was all pretty boring.

Five o'clock came at last. 'That's all for today,' Miss Trent said. She handed Dad two files. 'Read these tonight, Clipper.' She gave me an envelope. 'And Stevie, for your homework, arrange these notes for me.'

'Thanks,' I said.

'You're welcome. Tomorrow we go on two assignments.'

'Yes ma'am,' Dad said.

'They're straightforward assignments. All the assignments we'll have while you're training will be straightforward. I'll talk, you'll watch and learn, Rookie.' She meant Dad.

'Yes sir, ma'am,' Dad said.

This was more like it. I already felt I wasn't cut out for office life.

Chapter 12

Back home that evening, we read Miss Trent's files. We read them five times. Dad was determined to do his very best as a trainee, and then we might actually get to Mexico.

Miss Trent's first assignment was with Wade Slade, a rock star from way back when. Tomorrow morning he was pitching a new song to Harry Canter, the boss of Deep Groove Records. Miss Trent would help him remember the words of his song. Wade Slade, sometimes he forgot stuff.

The second assignment was with Sharon Fly,

a preschool teacher. An inspector was visiting Sharon Fly's preschool, and she was nervous. She needed Miss Trent's support teaching the kids a clap-handies song.

I put tomorrow's notes in order, and folded them back into the envelope.

CASE RT24A/Slade-Wade

Next morning, Thursday, Miss Trent located us to Wade Slade's shoulder, where he waited in Deep Groove's recording studio. I handed Miss Trent her notes, and she checked them once, twice, three times.

'I'll sing the first minute,' she said. 'Once we get him going, he'll remember the rest.' She had copycatted the voice of Wade Slade's favourite singer, the legendary DD Rex, into the locator.

She was ready.

'Okay, Wade?' Harry Canter called through the glass screen. Wade Slade nodded.

He was ready.

The backing track blared out.

Wade Slade jumped in the air like a jackknife, and Miss Trent's notes went flying. We only lost a second, and then we were back. Dad reorganised Miss Trent's notes and she sang in Wade Slade's ear.

Wade Slade hesitated a moment, and then crooned:

'Clap handies,

Clap handies,

Till Daddy comes home,

With sweets in his pocket,

For Baby alone.'

'Miss Trent!' I said. 'Stop!'

She was using the notes for Sharon Fly.

Miss Trent stopped all right, like she'd been hit by lightning.

Wade Slade stopped too. He listened back in his head to what he had just sung, and strummed his guitar a little.

'Follow your dreams, Wade Slade,' Dad whispered.

'You weren't expecting that, right?' Wade Slade said to Harry Canter. 'Me neither.' He strummed some more. 'Well, lots of the best songs... ' (Strum, strum) 'are about your baby... ' (D chord) 'all alone... ' (A chord) 'at home,' (another D chord).

He whanged out a brand new, just hatched song.

'Clap, shout, yell, whoop, Daddy's coming home,

Coming home Baby, to be with you alone.'

He sang those two lines again, and again.

'Man!' Harry Canter said. 'I wish we were recording this.'

'We are,' his junior said.

What I say is, if you Mess Up, you're in trouble. But if you follow that by doing Something Outstanding, you can make up for it. (In this case, Wade Slade followed up with an outstanding hit song, his first in twenty years.)

Next, we located to Sharon Fly's preschool. Miss Trent read the clap-handies song to Sharon, and Sharon repeated it, and the little wobbly kids joined in. (Later that week we heard that the inspector passed her with flying colours.)

'That was good,' I said. 'Everything worked out fine.'

But Miss Trent was shaken. We went back to the office, and Dad put on the kettle to make tea, just the way she liked it.

'I read the wrong notes,' she said. 'Nothing like that has ever happened to me before. And I mean nothing. And I mean never. This could mean a reprimand. For me! A reprimand!'

'You can blame me,' I said. 'Maybe I should have stapled the notes together.'

'And it turned out well,' Dad said, handing her a cup of tea. 'That's the main thing.'

'What was that you said to Wade Slade about a dream, Clipper?' Miss Trent said.

'I said *Follow your dreams*,' Dad said. 'I often say that. Humans need to hear it.'

'You can't talk to my humans,' Miss Trent said. 'You're a trainee.' She paused. 'Stevie, you can write the Wade Slade assignment report as part of your homework. Not too heavy on the detail, if you know what I mean.'

So I left out about Miss Trent's notes getting mixed up, and I focussed on Harry Canter saying, 'You got yourself a deal, Wade Slade! It's a privilege to have you on board.'

VITALLY IMPORTANT POINT
Being a perfectionist makes life hard.

Chapter 13

For the next week, me and Dad went on assignment with Miss Trent every day. She was picky, fussy, and committed heart and soul to the Minute Minder Department. She taught us a lot.

Then on Thursday, almost two weeks after me and Dad had started in the Minute Minder Department, Miss Trent told us that Sandra May would arrive in Tassimity that evening.

'At last!' I said. 'Let's hope she likes living with her Aunt Jane.'

'Yeah,' Dad said. 'And let's hope Aunt Jane likes

living with Sandra May.'

'Adults always like living with kids,' I said.

'That's true,' Dad said, although Miss Trent looked like it was news to her.

'Anyway,' Miss Trent said, 'we'll meet at their apartment tomorrow, 9 a.m.'

So next morning, right after breakfast, me and Dad located to Aunt Jane's apartment. Miss Trent arrived at exactly the same moment.

I had pictured Aunt Jane's apartment like ours, airy and bright, but it seemed a little run down, with worn out rugs, a dripping tap at the sink, and no shade on the ceiling light. Aunt Jane was sitting at the kitchen table. She was about Dad's age. Her hair was tied back tight from her face, and she was tapping at a computer. Sandra May was nowhere in sight.

We settled under a geranium on a kitchen shelf, and watched.

'What's she doing?' I said.

'She's an accountant,' Miss Trent said.

We were going to watch someone doing *sums*?

I fidgeted.

'Go look around,' Miss Trent whispered.

Good. I wanted to find Sandra May.

I sailed from the windowsill out to Aunt Jane's little square lobby, which was practically wall-to-wall doors. One door was ajar, and I floated in.

There was Sandra May, lying on a bed. Her loneliness filled the room and washed over me. Or maybe I imagined that. I went closer. She seemed different than in Linbradan. She was wearing washed-out, mismatched pyjamas, and I thought maybe she and the shower weren't on friendly terms. And her eyes had changed. Back then, they sparkled. Now they were dull.

I tried to listen to her flashing, splintered thoughts.

FLASH!

A family around a table, eating spaghetti.

FLASH!

Sandra May's bare feet picking across smooth, underwater stones.

FLASH!

Her bedroom curtains, covered with bluebells.

After a while Dad and Miss Trent joined me, and we listened to Sandra May's thoughts together.

'She's thinking about Linbradan all the time,' I whispered.

'I guess she's lonely for home,' Dad said.

'Poor child,' Miss Trent said. She looked at her watch. 'Time to go back to headquarters.'

In the office, Miss Trent started scheduling next week's minutes and writing them into the calendar. Cats, dogs, shopkeepers, students, a woman who was in hospital.

'What about Sandra May's minutes?' I said.

Miss Trent turned to me.

'I thought you understood, Stevie,' she said. 'I can't work with Sandra May. I have a backlog of assignments. And your dad can't work with her until he's trained. That's nearly three months away.'

'But she needs help now!' I said.

'So do all our people,' Miss Trent said. 'They have

to take their turn.'

'She only needs a friend,' I said. Maybe because that's what I thought about myself. 'If we could just find her a friend.'

'Unfortunately we can't,' Miss Trent said. 'But you can spend time with her, Stevie. You can watch, and listen, and get to know her.'

'Then we'll know what she needs when it's time for me to work with her,' Dad said. 'It'd be a big help.'

I didn't actually want to spend lots of time with Sandra May Bee. But I wanted to help Dad.

'Okay,' I said. 'I'll do it.'

Chapter 14

That evening after dinner me and Dad located to Sandra May's room. She looked miserable, slumped on her bed. There was a yellow teddy on her bedside table, and Dad had me sit in its lap, like it was an armchair.

'Just watch her thoughts,' Dad said. 'I'll go listen to Aunt Jane.'

I followed Sandra May's thoughts, which were mostly about Linbradan: an arrow of geese flying over the community centre, the giant beech shining by the bridge, the schoolyard with its redbrick walls. It was interesting, seeing Linbradan through her eyes.

After about an hour Dad collected me, and we located home.

'How was that?' he said.

'Okay, I guess,' I said. 'How about you?'

'Aunt Jane watched *Los Doctores,*' Dad said. 'I watched too, just to be polite.' He explained that *Los Doctores* was a TV soap, set in a Mexican hospital, where the staff and patients had extremely complicated and surprising lives.

'And Aunt Jane watches it?' I said. 'Really? A Mexican soap? Exactly what you'd like to watch?'

'Well, maybe I kind of suggested it when she was flicking through channels,' Dad said. 'It's educational.'

'It's not,' I said.

From then on we visited the Bees' apartment most evenings. Dad probably should have been studying, but pretty soon he and Aunt Jane were hooked on watching *Los Doctores*.

'It kind of *is* studying,' Dad said.

'It isn't,' I said.

'It shows how humans live and think.'

'It doesn't.'

I went where Sandra May went, which was usually her bedroom. It's hard to be with someone who's sad, when you can't help them. But I stuck with it.

Then one evening, about a week after Sandra May arrived in Tassimity, something different happened.

FLASH!

Sandra May remembered Linbradan River.
I remembered with her: the silky coolness, the peaty smell of the brown water, the glitter of sunshine.

I imagined floating on a raft, up to a gorse-covered hill.

Then Sandra May Bee *saw* my imagined raft!

Next, she remembered the birdsong over the gorse, and the stirring of grasses in the breeze. Then I felt the breeze, cool on my face, and she smiled with the feeling, and also she gave me the memory of the smell of rained-on earth. For a moment we both missed Linbradan together.

How did it happen? My theory is, imagining pictures is more powerful than thinking words, so my imagined raft whooshed straight into Sandra May's mind, even though my words couldn't. That's my theory anyhow.

Back home, I didn't tell Dad about it. Anyway,

he wanted to talk about *Los Doctores*. 'You won't believe what happened,' he said, shaking his head. 'That Nurse Gonzales is actually giving up nursing to become a surfer!'

'It's not real, Dad,' I said. Fidders don't have television, so sometimes we need reminding.

'Sure it's real. They just change the names. Why would anybody make that stuff up?'

I didn't answer. It might spoil his fun.

Every evening after that, without her knowing it, me and Sandra May imagined Linbradan together. We imagined market day, and the train swooshing through town. We remembered sitting in springtime fields, or climbing a bare tree under a sparkling winter sky. Imagining Linbradan made her feel a tiny bit better, although her heart ached even more to be back there, and so did mine.

Chapter 15

By now Dad was busy preparing for his first solo trainee assignment. A Minute Minder's first solo trainee assignment is almost always with a dog, because dogs will do pretty much anything to make somebody happy, human or fidder. Also, a first solo trainee assignment is simple enough to complete in one session – that is, in one minute.

CASE HC 51A/Hinckley-Gracie

This assignment was with Gracie Hinckley, a

handsome dog the colour of wheat. Gracie chewed her human's slippers and socks. Her human, Saul Hinckley, quite liked having slippers and socks. Dad had to persuade Gracie to stop the random chewing.

He keyed Gracie's address into the locator.

We were with Gracie. Dad switched on the translator. 'Gracie,' he said, 'those slippers are not for chewing. Those socks are not for chewing. Hey, girl, you got your own toys to chew.'

The translator told us out loud what Gracie was feeling.

'I can't resist the smell of Saul's feet.' The locator sensory function also let us smell Saul's feet, which I felt was unnecessary. But one of the rules of being a Minute

Minder, and it's a good rule, is that you have to accept your client's feelings.

'I know it's hard,' Dad said. 'But it would be practically impossible to train your human to tidy his things away. Pretty soon, he'll think you're a bad dog, and you'll be locked in the kitchen.'

Gracie thought some more. The locator screen showed us her thought-images, like a miniature cinema. In three seconds, Gracie saw herself locked in the kitchen away from Saul. She saw Saul in the living room, both of them lonely and apart, instead of snug as bugs on the couch together, watching television.

'I get it,' she thought at Dad. 'I'll stop chewing his stuff.'

Problem sorted.

'Excellent,' Dad said. 'And Gracie... follow your dreams.'

Gracie was puzzled.

'I live with Saul,' she said. 'The bestest, most gorgeousest human in the world. What's left to dream?'

We located back to headquarters, and Dad reported to Miss Trent.

'Not bad, Clipper,' she said. 'Your first solo assignment – and it only took half a minute.'

'Wasn't that an especially easy case?' I said. Miss Trent glared at me.

'Any case can go wrong,' she snapped, 'and this didn't.'

Dad looked chuffed. Maybe it was good to start on an easy case.

VITALLY IMPORTANT POINT
Sometimes baby steps work
better than giant strides.

Chapter 16

Back home, Dad started dinner, and I looked out across Beckett Park. A breeze cut the air, and bright kites coasted in the sky. I often watched the park, tracking kids playing together, and imagining being one of them.

'It's not a bad job, Minute Mindering,' Dad said from the kitchen area. He was grating carrots. 'Not bad at all.'

It was the first good thing he had ever said about being a Minute Minder, so I didn't remind him that he had to write a report, and fill in a time sheet, and categorise the half minute, and explain what he did with the other half.

In the park, one boy was cycling alone on his blue bike. He was about the same age as me and Sandra May. I saw him in the park almost every evening, sometimes alone, sometimes with his mother. And he seemed to emerge from behind our building, where humans locked their bikes.

Maybe he lived right here in Delvin Tower.

Maybe he wanted a friend.

A friend like Sandra May.

'Look, Dad,' I said, and Dad came to the window. 'That kid's always here,' I said, pointing. 'I think he lives in Delvin Tower.'

'Could be,' Dad said.

'How about we get to know him?' I said. 'Maybe we can bring him and Sandra May together.'

'I don't know what Miss Trent would say about that,' Dad said.

I do, I thought. But I said, 'She wouldn't have to know. It's your free time. I could write up your reports to make up. Please, Dad. Sandra May is real lonely.'

Dad considered. 'I can't think of an actual rule we'd be breaking,' he said. Not surprising, since he knew hardly any rules. 'Let's try it. Tell me when he leaves the park, and we'll join him.'

Dad went back to preparing dinner, and I kept watching the boy.

'He's leaving the park now, Dad!'

Dad took out the locator and keyed in some coordinates. I ran and linked arms with him, and *whirr* FIZZ ... we located right onto the boy's shoulder. We sat tight while he cycled around to the back of Delvin Tower, dismounted and locked his bike to a cycle stand. Then he walked back around to the street, and up the steps of Delvin Tower. Yes! He *did* live here.

We went up in the lift with him to floor 9. He let himself into 9-C, right beneath 10-C where Sandra May lived.

He called out, 'Hi, Mam.'

'Hi, Charlie!' His mother looked into the lobby. 'Wash your hands, pet, tea's just ready.' Charlie gave her a big, warm smile, and went into the bathroom.

Nice kid.

Perfect kid.

'He'd be an ace friend for Sandra May,' I said.

'If he wants,' Dad said.

Oh yeah. Charlie would have to actually want to be Sandra May's friend.

'Plus, how will they meet?' Dad said.

I had worked that out. 'Next time we see Charlie in the park, you can tell Aunt Jane to bring Sandra May there, to find her a friend. Then you can get them talking.'

'That might work,' Dad said. 'Maybe.'

The following evening I took up my post at the window. As soon as I spotted Charlie in the park, Dad located us to the Bees'. Aunt Jane and Sandra May were both on the sofa, reading. Dad whispered to Aunt Jane about going to the park and finding a friend for Sandra May.

'Yeah,' Aunt Jane thought back. 'Everyone needs a friend.'

'Now's a good time,' Dad whispered.

Aunt Jane looked at the clock. 'Hey, Sandra May,' she said. 'Will we go out for some fresh air?'

'Good work, Dad,' I said.

'Good work, Aunt Jane,' Dad said.

'No thanks,' Sandra May said. 'Tassimity air is *poison*.'

'Please?' Aunt Jane said. 'I'd like the company.'

Finally, Sandra May said okay, and they went to the park. Charlie and his mother were sitting on a bench, and Dad pointed them out to Aunt Jane.

'It's a bit scary,' Aunt Jane thought, 'just talking to someone you've never met.'

'Some things you do, even if you're scared,' Dad said.

Aunt Jane took a deep breath.

And in five minutes, which is no time at all for something wonderful to happen, she and Charlie's mother were talking and smiling.

Then Charlie gave Sandra May a go on his bike, and after that they took turns.

'Happy?' Dad said to me.

'For sure! Dad, you're the best.'

He grinned. 'It's easy when the humans want what you want.'

After his tea, Charlie visited Sandra May, and so did I. Me and Dad had helped them meet, but now Sandra May and Charlie became friends by themselves, mainly by talking. In just a few minutes they knew each other's favourite TV shows, and music, and foods. They found out they would be in the same class in Beckett School, starting next week.

I could hardly believe it. It was my first human case, and it had succeeded. Admittedly, Dad had done the actual work, and said the right words at the right time to Aunt Jane.

But still.

I had found
a friend for
Sandra May.

Chapter 17

The next evening, Sandra May and Charlie found two tin cans, and tied one to each end of a long, strong string. They hooked the string around Sandra May's window catch, so a tin dangled down at Charlie's window on the floor below. When they tugged one tin, the other tin rattled, showing they wanted to send something up or down. Sandra May tried it out by sending a badge with a lilac-coloured cat down to Charlie. Her brother Ben had given it to her, and now she wanted Charlie to have it.

A couple of days later Aunt Jane bought a second-hand yellow bike for Sandra May. That afternoon Sandra May and Charlie cycled in the park together, and went to the playground. Sandra May swarmed up the climbing frame in an instant.

Charlie said, 'Sandra May is like a cat. Shimmies up, just like that.'

'Woah, Charlie!' Sandra May said. 'You're a poet!'

Charlie glanced around. 'Can you keep a secret, Sandra May?'

She swung herself back to ground level. 'Sure.'

'I do write poems,'
he whispered.

'Why is that a secret?'

'Some people think it's lame.'

'Well,' Sandra May said, 'I'm your friend and I think it's brilliant.'

Just then she noticed a signpost.

'Look, Charlie. There's an actual cycle track in the park!'

'We can't go there,' Charlie said. 'It's way over the other side.'

'Sure, we can!' Sandra May said. 'Come on!'

She set off, with me and Dad on her shoulder. Charlie cycled slowly after us.

At the cycle track Sandra May and Charlie dismounted to wheel their bikes in. But a big kid stepped in front of the gate, blocking them.

'What are you doing here, Charlie Tobin?' he said. Charlie backed away. 'You know this is my side of the park.'

'It's not *your* side of the park,' Sandra May said. 'It's everyone's!'

'No it isn't,' the boy said. 'Right, Tobin?'

Charlie didn't answer.

'*Right,* Tobin?'

'Yes, Badger,' Charlie said, very quiet.

'That's crazy!' Sandra May said.

'Careful, Twinkle-Toes.' Badger kicked dust on one of Sandra May's sparkly sandals. 'Any friend of Tobin's is an enemy of mine.'

'Let's go, Sandra May.' Charlie started wheeling his bike away, and after a moment, full of anger, Sandra May followed.

'We shouldn't let that Badger push us around, Charlie!'

'Don't annoy him,' Charlie said. 'He'll ruin your life. He bullied me in school all last year.'

'He's in our school?' Sandra May said.

'In our actual class,' Charlie said. 'You know Tip Top Bakes? On O'Malley Street, north side of the park? That's where he lives. Keep away from him, is my advice.'

And slowly, thinking their different thoughts, they wheeled their bikes back towards home.

When we went to the Bees' that evening, Charlie was visiting. He and Sandra May watched *Los Doctores* with Aunt Jane. Me and Dad watched too, sitting together on Sandra May's pencil case. When Charlie went home Dad stayed with Aunt Jane and I followed Sandra May to her room. She lay on her bed, with her legs up the wall, thinking. I lay beside her, and put my legs up the wall too. It was relaxing.

FLASH! Plump blackberries bursting juice into her mouth.

FLASH! Nurse Gonzales winning her surfing competition.

FLASH! Linbradan River.

I sensed that she was remembering things she liked, to sidestep thoughts of Badger.

Wait – I sensed that?

I felt a tickle of excitement.

Up until now, I couldn't sense anything about a human. I just heard their words and thoughts. Now I sensed Sandra May was a mix of angry and anxious about Badger, without her actually thinking it. I sensed she was glad to be friends with Charlie, but longed for Linbradan. Was I developing a new skill, just by listening and watching carefully?

FLASH! Her new yellow bike.

FLASH! Her sparkly sandals.

'I love those sandals,' I said lazily.

FLASH! I heard what she heard — me, like a

buzzing fly.

She scratched her arm.

'I would love sandals like those,' I continued.

Buzz, buzz, we both heard. She scratched some more, as though hearing me gave her an allergy.

I suddenly realised what I was doing – talking to a human, after everything I had been told!

I stopped talking, and just stayed by her, our four legs up the wall.

FLASH! Remembering Badger kicking dust at her sandal.

FLASH! Imagining pushing him into the park pond.

A rattling at the window made Sandra May jump up. She leaned out and pulled up the tin can. Charlie had sent her up a piece of candy. She grinned, and so did I. She put it in her mouth, and we both tasted strawberry.

Chapter 18

'Today's assignment is with Sully Sullivan,' Dad said. It was Monday morning, two days later. 'A spaniel. I have to tell him to stop licking his private parts.'

'Don't all dogs do that?' I asked.

'Pretty much,' Dad said. 'And all their humans seem to want them to stop.'

CASE HC84N/Sullivan-Sully

We located to Camberwell Square East, where Sully Sullivan lived. There were six little houses each side of the square, with jumbles of gardens behind.

The locator bipped. 'Darn,' Dad said. 'Low battery. Only a minute left.' For once I had forgotten to charge the locator. Dad switched it off to save the battery for talking to Sully.

'Come on,' he said. 'Sully lives in number 3.' He floated up to the third house, and I followed. Some human kids were playing ball right outside, using sweaters for goal posts.

'There's no number on the house,' I said. 'Can we check it's Sully's? One of those kids will know.'

Dad paid no attention. He is one hundred percent one of those fidders who would walk in circles for a month before asking for directions.

'Look,' he said, 'that window's open.' He flitted to the windowsill and slipped in, and I followed.

Inside, lying on his back and snoring, was Sully. He was cute. He was scruffy.

He was mainly white, with pointy black ears and a tan patch over one eye. Dad switched on the locator and clicked to translator.

'A message for you,' Dad thought at Sully. Sully stretched and opened one eye. 'You got to stop licking your private parts in public,' Dad said. 'It embarrasses your human.'

'Me?' Sully thought back at Dad.

Eight seconds.

I saw the dog's name tag.

'Dad.'

'Quiet, Stevie.'

'Wrong dog, Dad.'

Dad looked properly. 'You're not a spaniel, are you?'

'No.' The dog sat up and stretched.

'You're a terrier.'

'You're a genius.'

'And your name is...'

'Tammy. Sully lives next door.'

Twenty-four seconds.

'This isn't number three?' Dad said. 'We counted!'

'You counted from the wrong end of the street. This is number four.' Tammy scratched an ear.

Thirty seconds.

'And yeah,' Tammy went on, 'that's a habit of Sully's, licking his private parts. You're saying it's a problem?'

'The problem is his human don't like it,' Dad said. 'And darn it, the other problem is I've used up forty seconds.'

Dad would be in trouble. Unless...

'Ask Tammy to pass the message on to Sully,' I said to Dad.

'Good thinking,' Dad said. 'Tammy, can you give our message to Sully?'

'Sure,' Tammy thought.

'You can?' Dad said.

'Trust me,' Tammy thought. 'I'm a dog.'

Before the locator battery went completely flat, Tammy agreed to let Dad put a Monitor Tab on her ear.

A Monitor Tab is a tiny camera, smaller than my little fingernail. Tammy's Monitor Tab was linked to Dad's locator. So that afternoon, we watched Tammy

give Sully our message, over their garden fence.

'You gotta stop licking like that, Sully,' Tammy said. 'Your human doesn't like it.'

'For real?' Sully said. He was drop-dead gorgeous, with glossy fur and floppy ears.

'Yeah, for real.'

'Ohhh-kay.' Sully raised his glorious spaniel eyes to heaven.

And that was it. Mission accomplished. Life was a breeze, working with dogs.

However, Dad had gone to the wrong house.

We thought nobody saw.

But somebody always sees.

The Minute Minder Department doled out reprimands if you made mistakes. It helped them complete more work, despite staff shortages.

This time, Miss Trent had us arrange all her files in alphabetical order, instead of by date. I did it as part of my schooling, and to help Dad. I hummed all through it, full up with feel-good after meeting Tammy.

VITALLY IMPORTANT POINT

It's worth asking someone you trust for help. and you can usually trust a dog.

Chapter 19

Two days later, Wednesday, was Sandra May's first day in Beckett School. That morning the clouds rolled in. Me and Dad gathered our laundry from the balcony, rain pitching down on us. Then we located to the office and sat, shivery and damp, rain snailing down the windowpane. Miss Trent was dry as an indoor cat. I looked at this month's calendar picture: palm trees, bright blue sea, white sand as fine as sifted flour.

'Clipper,' Miss Trent said. I turned my attention back to her. 'Your Minute Minder exam is coming up.'

'Yes, ma'am,' Dad said.

'Face it,' Miss Trent said. 'You'll fail.'

'Seriously?' Dad said, although we both knew that, if Miss Trent had a fault, and we would never tell her she had one, it was that she was always serious.

'You're a good Minute Minder,' Miss Trent said. 'In fact, you're a natural in the field. If it was all about our clients being happy, it would work out perfect. But there are rules, Clipper. You just won't learn the rules.'

She had him there.

'You have me there, Miss Trent,' Dad said.

'And if you won't learn the rules, you can't obey the rules,' Miss Trent continued, just as though Dad would have obeyed the rules if he knew them.

I didn't want to think about Dad losing another job, even one he didn't much like. Instead, I imagined walking barefoot on that calendar beach. Before I knew it, I was imagining walking with Sandra May Bee. She was carrying her twinkling sandals, and squealing at the heat of the sand.

We ran to the sea to cool our feet. I didn't know if I was as big as a human, or if she was as small as a fidder. We were just kids, and we were friends.

'Well, Stevie?' Miss Trent said.

'Sorry?'

'I said, I came across a new rule last night.' A new rule! What could be more thrilling? 'It's in an old Statutes Book, which predates our rulebooks.' She beamed at us, like we might have a clue what she was talking about.

A statute, it seems, is an actual law, a rule that

trumps other rules. The statute Miss Trent found said:

> *If a Minute Minder Trainee's career is being unreasonably obstructed due to an extensive waiting list for the Rules Examination, said Minute Minder Trainee can claim the right to do an Appropriate Practical Test in lieu. If they pass, the Examination is waived, and a Licence Amnesty is granted.*

'Get it?' Miss Trent said.

Dad was frowning as though Miss Trent was speaking Martian. I didn't understand most of what she said, but I thought I understood one bit.

'Dad wouldn't have to do an exam?' I said.

'Precisely,' Miss Trent said. Dad positively glowed when he heard this. 'You see, currently there is a huge backlog of trainees waiting to do the examination,' Miss Trent went on, 'because three different examiners have to correct the paper in triplicate.' For once it was in Dad's favour that Minute Minders overdo the paperwork.

'So I can skip the exams?' he said.

'On the condition,' Miss Trent read from the statute again, 'That you complete an Appropriate Practical Test, to be commissioned by the Departmental Chief.'

'Yes, please, thanks,' Dad said.

Miss Trent said the Chief needed to agree. He was, she said, a tricky customer, especially if his golf swing was off. But she thought she could persuade him. We had never met the Chief, but I believed her.

Another supervisor would probably have failed Dad on day one. Miss Trent talked tough, and she acted tough, but she kept faith with Dad all the way.

VITALLY IMPORTANT POINT
Keep faith with your humans,
and with your fidders.

Chapter 20

We located to Sandra May before dinner because, I told Dad, I couldn't eat until I knew how her first day at school had been.

Dad left me with her and went to watch *Los Doctores* with Aunt Jane. (One of the doctors was trapped in a goldmine. It was nail-biting stuff.)

I watched Sandra May's thoughts.

She felt overwhelmed by Beckett School, with its masses of kids. (There had only been fifty kids in Linbradan School.)

But her desk was beside Charlie. Good.

She liked her new navy shoes. Good.

Badger cornered her at lunchtime. Bad.

He said, 'If it isn't Twinkle-Toes! Still hanging out with my enemy, Tobin? You're looking for trouble.'

Lying on her bed now, Sandra May brooded about Badger. At break time he had handed round Tip Top

Bakes ginger cookies. Badger often brought cookies in, another kid told her.

Now on her bed she thought, 'That's probably why some kids like him, because he brings cookies in, and because he's a football star.'

After a while, Charlie visited, and they played a board game called *Fight or Flight*.

Maybe school would be okay, I thought, if Sandra May and Charlie could keep away from Badger.

A few evenings later, Dad was matching his socks into pairs, one of his favourite jobs. 'Why not visit Sandra May on your own?' he said. 'You got to use the locator solo sometime, Stevie.'

From when they're nine, fidder kids can locate solo. I never had. Probably because of Mom and Dicey and Annie vanishing. Even though I pictured the three of them snoozing and dreaming in their shiny duvet cloud, I didn't want to disappear myself.

But I wanted to visit Sandra May Bee.

'Okay,' I whispered. Dad looked surprised. His little Stevie, all growed up. Growed up a small bit, anyway.

'Well, good,' he said. 'Are you sure?' I wasn't, but I nodded. Dad set the locator, and handed it to me. It was smooth and weighty. Was I ready to do this on my own? I took a breath, looked at Dad and pressed locate. Dad fogged in front of my eyes.

I opened my eyes...

Yes! I had located solo to Sandra May's room. The relief! I mentally patted myself on the back. I would never worry again about disappearing. Or at least not so much.

Charlie was in Sandra May's room. He often

visited after finishing his homework.

'What's your homework poem about?' Sandra May said. 'Mine's about Linbradan. River, quiver, shiver.'

'My poem's stupid,' Charlie said. 'I don't even *know* what it's about.'

'I bet it's *brilliant*.'

'It definitely isn't.'

Next evening I located solo to Sandra May again. It was easy-peasy. A snap.

Sandra May was on her own this time, and her thoughts were jagged and painful. I watched and listened carefully, and pieced together what had turned into a very bad day.

It started okay. During creative writing class, Charlie asked could he rewrite his homework poem and read it tomorrow instead. Ms Carbury said, 'No problem, Charlie.'

Then at breaktime, Badger snatched Charlie's homework notebook, clambered onto the yard wall, and shouted out Charlie's poem. Sandra May was so swamped with anger and fear I couldn't hear the poem, just her *Dah-de-dah*.

'Catch, Bunny-Boy!' Badger threw the notebook to Charlie and jumped off the wall, crashing against Sandra May. 'Twinkle-Toes, your friend Bunny-Boy is a loser!'

Sandra May's arm throbbed where Badger had banged into her. Would he never leave her alone? Couldn't Charlie stand up for himself? No, she thought, Charlie isn't that kind of kid.

I could feel Sandra May trying not to remember what she did next, and to make her mind go *dah-de-dah*. But the memory forced itself in.

She remembered saying, 'Charlie's not my friend.'

Then she remembered Charlie's face, white and frozen. He took a step back, and walked away. He seemed to have shrunk. Inside, Sandra May felt like she was crumbling.

They didn't speak for the rest of the day.

Now, on her bed, Sandra May was quiet as fog.

Then something rattled. Sandra May went to the window, drew the tin can up and turned it over. The badge with the lilac cat, the one her brother Ben had given to Sandra May, fell out.

There was a note, too. It said: *You should have told me we weren't friends.*

Sandra May felt so wretched she couldn't move. She was even sadder than when she first came to Tassimity. She had betrayed her only friend, and she was all alone again, and so was Charlie.

I felt wretched too. What should I do?

Obvious, really.

Bring on the head honcho, I thought. Bring on Hal Clipper. He'll know how to sort this out. I pressed the locator home key.

But as soon as he saw me, Dad said, 'Guess what, Stevie?'

He held up a file. 'My APT arrived!'

'Oh,' I said. 'Great.'

'I know!' Dad said. 'I'm gonna study it inside-out. This could be the most crucial assignment of my life. I won't even have time to watch *Los Doctores*.'

Yes. Dad's APT was so important he wouldn't have a minute to help Sandra May. She would go on being miserable and lonely, and so would Charlie. There was nothing I could do. Absolutely nothing.

Unless...

Yes.

Maybe.

Maybe I could help her fix things with Charlie, and become the human she was deep down.

In fact, the way I saw it, I had no choice.

It was time to become a criminal. An outlaw. A very, very bad fidder kid.

It was time for me to talk to Sandra May.

Chapter 21

I crept into Dad's bedroom and searched his bookshelves until I found a nondescript little book: *Communicating with Your Human* by Prof Mo Ryan. I smuggled it to my bedroom and started reading.

It turns out it is annoyingly simple to talk to humans.

Prof Mo Ryan's first main point: *Imagine actually being your human. Echo their body language with your own. The more you do this, the clearer an echo of them you find in yourself. We call this Empathy Echo.*

First you imagine *being* them, and *then* you talk

to them.

Prof Mo Ryan said not to skip forward.

I skipped forward.

Second main point: *Then, listening carefully all the time, you talk to them.*

I'd be good at this empathy echo listening thing. I'd go back right now and talk to Sandra May. I stuck the book under my sweater and went out to Dad.

'Can I go see Sandra May again, Dad?'

'Huh?' He was still puzzling over his APT. 'Sure. Dinner in twenty minutes.'

Sandra May was curled on her bed like a periwinkle, her mind a jungle of today's miserable memories.

I curled up too, and spent some time checking I was echoing her body.

Then I spoke to her, using my own voice. I didn't know how to use the copycat function.

'You'll be braver next time, Sandra May.'

Sandra May heard the usual buzzing when I spoke, but this time she almost heard a couple of my words too.

Buzz, neck-time, buzz.

'You can be friends with Charlie again.'

Buzz, fren-zwit, buzz, buzz.

Sandra May felt irritated. So did I.

She scratched her arm. I scratched mine.

She thought maybe she was hallucinating. I knew she wasn't.

This wasn't working. I sat up and took *Communicating with Your Human* out from under my sweater, and opened it at the bit that said not to skip forward. Sandra May stopped scratching, and sighed.

A sure-fire way to stymie the process is to give advice before your human is ready.

I didn't know what stymie meant. But maybe Sandra May wasn't ready for my advice.

It was dinnertime. I located home, hungry. Dad was surveying his APT photos, and I felt a twist of guilt. We usually talked his assignments through together. And this one was so important.

He looked up and smiled. 'Dinner in five,' he said.

I washed my hands, put *Communicating with Your Human* back in Dad's bedroom, and looked up 'stymie' in the dictionary.

Oh.

Dinner was beans on toast. I eyed Dad while waiting for my beans to cool down a little. He looked in a good mood.

'Can I ask you something?' I said.

'Sure.'

'Is it hard to talk to humans?'

Dad ground salt onto his beans. 'Yes.'

'I notice you often echo their body language,' I lied.

'Really?' Dad looked interested.

'I just don't want to stymie things when I'm older,' I explained.

Dad put the saltcellar down.

'Stevie, who's been telling you about talking to humans?'

Oh. That wasn't an 'I'm interested' look, it was a 'what are you hiding?' look. I shouldn't have said 'stymie'. Dad probably read it in *Communicating with Your Human*. Probably the only darn sentence he read in the whole book.

'Nobody,' I said. 'No way.'

'Well, what? Shoot. Tell me what you know, and how you know it.'

'I read a bit about it in one of your study books,' I said, truthfully. 'Kind of by accident,' I said, less truthfully.

'Give me patience.' Dad's fingers were angled and tense on the table. 'No more reading my study books. Especially anything about talking to humans.'

'Okay.'

'I can't afford to lose another job.'

'I won't do it again, Dad.'

'Promise?'

'Promise.'

I felt relieved, in a funny way. Sandra May Bee, she had her Aunt Jane, and her mother and father and brothers, and she would probably be back with them in Linbradan in a few lousy months.

I just had Dad.

'Sorry, Sandra May Bee,' I thought. 'You'll have to work things out for yourself. I'm done with you.'

But in bed that night, looking at the ceiling, I thought about Sandra May, in her own bed, probably looking at the ceiling too. She was ten, like me. And without Charlie, she had no friends. Just like me.

I wouldn't read Dad's books any more. I didn't

always keep promises, but I would keep this one. Still, I had read some of *Communicating with Your Human,* so I now knew something about talking to them. Maybe enough to talk to Sandra May Bee, and be her actual friend.

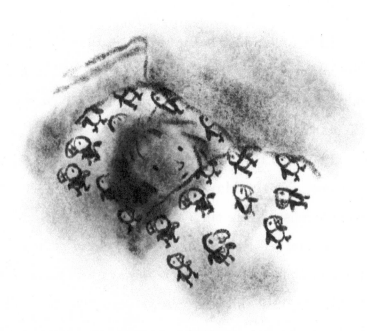

Chapter 22

Miss Trent's office, next morning.

'So, Clipper, whaddayathink of your APT?'

'Exciting,' Dad said.

'And you, Stevie?'

'I haven't read it yet.'

'Slipping up, Stevie.' She pointed at Dad. 'Summarise it for her, Clipper.'

'It's with Charlie Tobin,' Dad told me.

'He lives right in our building!' I said to Miss Trent.

Miss Trent said, 'That's precisely why the Chief put your dad on this assignment.'

Dad showed me Charlie's photo. My heart ached to think of him in school today, with Sandra May being his not-friend.

'And wait for it...' Dad said. 'The assignment is from the Art Department!'

'No way!' I said. Me and Dad had always wanted to work with the Art Department.

I'm not sure I understand exactly how the Art Department works, but here's the basics.

HOW THE ART DEPARTMENT WORKS

Ideas for paintings, books, songs, poems – all kinds of art – they all exist in a sort of dream world. They journey around, looking for a human to make them into real art. If the idea doesn't find a human pretty quickly, it arrives in the Art Department.

La la la, not listening.

Maybe later...
I'm too busy.

Boring idea.

ART DEPARTMENT

Then the Art Department matches the idea with a human artist, and the human makes the idea into art.

ARTISTS WAITING FOR IDEAS

'There's a poem,' Dad said. 'Poem CT435. And it's matched to Charlie, because he's a poet.'

I flicked through the file.

Last Monday, an Art Department Executive, Alfie MacTalfie, gave poem CT435 to Charlie. But something went wrong.

'I wonder why Charlie didn't write this gosh-darned poem?' Dad said.

'But he did,' I said, remembering Badger shouting out Charlie's poem from the yard wall. 'And like the file says, it went wrong.'

I riffled through the file, and stopped at this

sentence: *'Further confidential details for narrative disclosure only'.*

'What's that mean?' I said.

'It means there's something Alfie MacTalfie didn't write down,' Miss Trent said. 'He'll only tell you face to face.'

'Why?'

'How would I know?' Miss Trent said.

'Here's the poem,' Dad said, passing a sheet of paper to me.

This lean, grey fox
Shivers the forest air.
We shrink from her,
This loving mother.

Which of us will feed her young?

'Ooh,' I said. 'That's a bit...'

'Dark,' Miss Trent said. 'Yes, well, that's not your problem. Clipper, you have three minutes in total on your APT. This is a complex assignment.' She shook his hand. 'Good luck. I have high hopes for you.'

That evening, I cleared up after a Mexican style dinner, and Dad read his APT file again. My mouth still burned from the black bean burritos. Dad sometimes went a little heavy on the chilli.

'See, we have a kid who likes writing poems,' Dad said, 'and a poem that wants to be written. Easy.'

'And Alfie MacTalfie can explain what went wrong the first time,' I said. 'In his narrative disclosure thing.' I put our two plates back in the cupboard.

'No need,' Dad said breezily. 'We actually know Charlie, that gives us the edge. It's a five-line poem! How hard can it be?' He looked perilously confident.

'You'll find out when you call Alfie

MacTalfie,' I said. Two knives and two forks in the drawer. 'You need to call him.'

'Nah,' Dad said. 'We'll sail through.' He started whistling, and checking through Charlie's audio files.

I told Dad about how Charlie told Sandra May he wrote a bad poem, and about Badger calling him Bunny-Boy, and all that.

Dad didn't listen. He copycatted the booming voice of Charlie's football coach into the locator, whistling all the while.

He was oh so smart.

He was oh so experienced.

He was oh so deluded.

Inside I was groaning. I wasn't sure when Dad became the reckless one instead of me. Maybe when we moved to Tassimity. Or maybe he had always been a bit reckless, and I just didn't see it. But by now I knew that when Hal Clipper was this confident, someone needed to duck for cover.

Chapter 23

At 7.40 p.m., Dad clicked Charlie Tobin's co-ordinates into the locator, and *whirr* FIZZ... we were in his home.

CASE HC32L/Tobin-Charlie

Charlie was sitting in a large olive-green chair, gazing into space. He looked as bleak as it was possible for a ten-year-old human to look. Dad glided onto his shoulder, and I followed.

 Minute 1

Dad took Poem CT435 from his backpack, cleared his throat, and proclaimed the first line. Charlie heard his football coach bellow out,

'This lean, grey fox...'

Charlie sat bolt upright, like he'd been jabbed with a pin. He put his hands over his ears, and started shout-singing.

There WAS an old woman
Who LIVED in the woods
Weel-ya Weel-ya WALL-ya
There WAS an old woman LA LA LA

Well, that didn't work.

In a daze, me and Dad located home. I wrote the word 'Exploratory' in 'Purpose for Minute' on Charlie's file.

'I messed up.' Dad sounded sorry, which didn't mean he would do it right next time. But it wouldn't help to say this, and I didn't. 'Darn. I wanted to tell him to follow his dream and be a poet again.'

'We only have two more minutes,' I said. 'You have to talk to this Alfie MacTalfie guy.'

'Aw, sheesh,' Dad said. No way did Hal Clipper want to ask for help. But I was determined that Dad would pass his APT, and that we would help Charlie. Charlie's problems and Sandra May's tangled together in my head, and I wanted to untangle things for both

157

of them.

'Let me ring him tomorrow morning,' I said. 'We're missing something. Maybe Charlie hates his football coach. Maybe he's allergic to foxes.'

'Aw, sheesh,' Dad said again. He sulked. He said he didn't want to go to see Sandra May, or Aunt Jane, and he didn't want to watch *Los Doctores*. He had had enough of humans for one evening, thank you very much.

So I located solo, ready to try talking to Sandra May again.

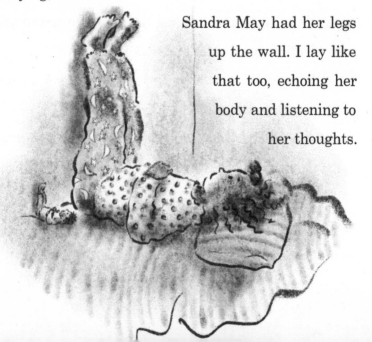

Sandra May had her legs up the wall. I lay like that too, echoing her body and listening to her thoughts.

FLASH! A memory from today, Sandra May and Charlie sitting apart in class. I felt the crush of her loneliness.

I remembered what I read in the book yesterday, before dinner. Did I know enough now to talk to her? I calmed my breathing.

'Charlie must miss you too,' I said.

Sandra May Bee heard.

Charlie must miss you too.

She heard it as a faint, whispered thought of her own, but in my voice.

My hands gripped into fists. Would she think this was weird?

But humans are used to random thoughts that sound like they come from someone else, and it seemed natural to Sandra May.

'No,' she thought back. 'Charlie must hate me.'

I had done it!

I had spoken to Sandra May Bee, and she had answered!

I was the first fidder kid ever to talk to humans.

I was a genius.

But I couldn't just sit here, congratulating myself. I had to talk to Sandra May.

'I bet he doesn't hate you,' I said.

She heard me again, that light, distant whisper. She considered.

'Maybe,' she thought. 'Maybe Charlie's too nice to *hate* me. But he knows I'm horrible.'

'But you're nice, Sandra May,' I said, my voice stronger in her head. Already I was sensing how to direct it to the part of the brain humans hear with.

'Oh yeah? It's nice to be a scaredy-cat chicken who abandons her friend?'

'You're nice, deep down,' I said.

It so happens I think pretty much all humans are nice, deep down. Some you have to go deeper to find the nice, is all.

Sandra May sat up. 'Who are you?' she thought. 'Who's talking to me?'

I was prepared for that.

'My name's Stevie,' I said. 'I'm your imaginary friend.'

'Woah!' Sandra May said. 'Okay. I suppose that makes sense, since no actual *real* person wants to be my friend.'

'You can have real friends and imaginary ones,' I said. 'Although your real friends like Charlie need you more than your imaginary ones.'

She wasn't listening.

'I know just what you look like, Stevie.' I saw how she imagined I looked, and let me tell you it was nothing like the real me. But she gave me twinkly sandals like hers, which was nice.

'You have a really good imagination,' I said. 'That's a big plus in life, in my opinion. Go on, imagine some more about me.'

'You're a friend all the way from Linbradan,' Sandra May thought. 'So now we can talk about home!'

'And I miss Linbradan, like you do, right?'

'Right!'

We talked about things we missed from Linbradan: midsummer festival, the wooded hills behind the town, how everyone knew your name, and especially we both missed the river.

I didn't talk to her any more about Charlie. I would do that bit by bit, listening carefully, like the book said.

'My imaginary friend, Stevie,' Sandra May thought. 'Well. An imaginary friend's better than no friend at all.'

Yes, I thought to myself. It is.

Chapter 24

Next morning, I rang Alfie MacTalfie's number from our apartment.

A voice yelled, 'YEAH?'

Alfie MacTalfie, my brilliant mind told me. He had to yell to be heard over the hullabaloo behind him.

'Mr MacTalfie?' I yelled back.

'Who wants to know?'

'Stevie Clipper. I'm calling for my dad, Hal Clipper. Seeking further information on Poem CT435.'

There was a brief pause.

'Well?' Alfie MacTalfie said.

'You wrote that you have *further confidential details for narrative disclosure only*,' I said. 'What details, please?'

'You want more information, you meet me. With I.D.'

'For sure, you name the place, Mr MacTalfie. You got time to meet us today, Mr MacTalfie?'

'I got time.' He suggested we meet in twenty minutes, in Honey's Diner. 'You prob'ly know it,' he said. 'It's right around the corner from your crummy Minute Minder Department.'

Me and Dad located to outside Honey's Diner. A steady drizzle greyed the air. We must have passed Honey's Diner a hundred times before without noticing it. I pushed the door open, and a bell tinged. A brown-haired, brown-eyed woman was stacking cups behind the counter. She must be Honey.

'Coffee?' she said to Dad.

'Sure thing,' Dad said. 'Are you Honey?'

'Yep,' she said.

Boy, I should have
been a detective.

'And for you, kid?'

'Hot chocolate,
please.'

'We're meeting
someone here,' Dad said.
'Maybe you know him,
name of Alfie MacTalfie?'

'You poor sap,' Honey said. 'Yeah, I know him. Sit
anywhere you like.'

I picked a window table that had a tablecloth
patterned with palm trees. The glass was misted over
with the damp day. Blurry shapes passed outside,
fidder and human. Dad sat beside me, leaving space
for Alfie MacTalfie opposite.

Honey strolled down with our drinks. I gripped
my mug of hot chocolate to warm my hands, and
Honey went back behind the counter and started
shining cutlery.

The door tinged again, and a squat man barrelled in. His tie looked like it might choke him, set at the top of his short neck.

'Howdy, Honey,' he called.

'By the window, MacTalfie,' she said, without looking up.

He lifted a stubby arm to salute us. 'You the rookie?' he said. Dad nodded. Honey was already bringing coffee for Alfie MacTalfie, and he gave her a goofy 'I have a crush on you' smile.

'Gimme a snack, Honey,' he said, and sat down across the table from us. 'The usual.'

The usual turned out to be a chocolate muffin, a bagel with avocado, and a plain doughnut.

We waited while Alfie MacTalfie munched the bagel, then the muffin, gulped his coffee, and pointed to his mug for a refill to have with the doughnut. Then he undid his belt a notch and looked at Dad. 'How can I help, Rookie?' he said.

166

'You want to see our I.D.?' I said.

'Sure, I do,' he said. 'You think I forgot? I'm a professional.'

This Alfie MacTalfie was a sensitive little flower.

We showed him our I.D. 'I wouldn't have told you nothing without I saw that first,' he said. Then Dad took Charlie Tobin's file from his backpack. Alfie MacTalfie looked at it like it was infectious.

'I started reading the poem to Charlie Tobin last night,' Dad said, 'and he went plumb crazy. What's his problem?'

Alfie MacTalfie puffed out his cheeks and glanced around.

'This is off the record,' he said. 'Agreed?'

We nodded.

Alfie MacTalfie put two fingers inside his tie and wiggled some breathing space. 'So. Monday, three days ago, I get this file, right?'

We nodded. Honey refilled Dad and Alfie's coffee

cups, then leaned on the counter and listened along with us.

'It's a poem. *This Lean Grey Fox*, that's the first line. And I'm reading it right here in Honey's, yeah? Before I go to Charlie Tobin's place?'

We nodded.

'And next thing – the poem's covered in jam.' He shifted in his seat, splashing coffee on the file. 'I don't know how it happened.'

We nodded again, and I moved the file to safety.

'But now I could only read the first line.' We nodded some more. I felt like one of those nodding toys in the back of a car.

'I didn't make a copy of the original poem,' Alfie said. 'So now there wasn't any poem left. Just the first line.'

Alfie McTalfie glared at us.

We nodded.

'So...' he looked at his fingernails. They weren't

clean. 'I wrote the rest.'

'You're a poet?' Dad said.

'Naw, but what else could I do?'

We didn't nod.

Alfie MacTalfie had written a new poem, right there in Honey's. That was the poem he read to Charlie Tobin. That was the poem Charlie Tobin wrote for homework.

'Next day, Tuesday, Charlie goes to school,' Alfie MacTalfie said. 'Another kid reads the poem in front of everyone.' Alfie MacTalfie shook his head and gulped some coffee.

I recalled Sandra May's memory of the whole miserable incident as clearly as if I had been there.

'I liked my poem,' Alfie MacTalfie said. 'There were things in it kids like. Foxes and bunny-wunnies.'

So that was why Badger started shouting *Bunny-Boy* at Charlie.

'You put *bunny-wunnies* in?' Dad said, awestruck.

'Yeah, so what?'

We were silent a moment.

'So last night,' I said, 'Dad read the first line of the poem, and it brought back terrible memories to Charlie.'

'I guess,' Alfie MacTalfie said. 'Also, Charlie Tobin hasn't actually written the *real* poem, just my *fake* poem. I'm off the case now, and it's a big FAIL in my record.'

'Can we hear your poem, Mr MacTalfie?' Dad said.

'No.'

'I think we need to,' I said. 'We need to know what we're up against.'

'No.'

'Maybe you don't remember it?' Dad said.

'I wish,' Alfie said gloomily. 'I really wish I didn't remember it. Okay, here goes.'

He lowered his voice so we had to lean across the table to hear.

This lean grey fox
Is sitting on a box

He wants a bunny-wunny to eat.

The bunny-wunny runs away

What a happy day

But the fox has very hungry feet.'

'Feet?' Dad said. 'Hungry feet?'

'It was to make it rhyme,' Alfie MacTalfie said.

'Poems don't have to rhyme,' I said.

'Yeah, yeah,' Alfie MacTalfie said. 'Everyone *says* that. But we all like it better when they do.' He spooned more sugar into his coffee. 'When my poem bombed, a colleague wrote another poem for me, using the original first line. *This lean, grey, fox.'*

'So now there are three *'Lean grey fox'* poems?' I said. 'The one that got jam on it, the one you wrote, and your colleague's? And that's the one Dad read last night?'

'Complicated, right?' Alfie MacTalfie said.

'You're allowed change poems?' Dad said.

'They all start the same,' Alfie MacTalfie said defensively.

Honey came down and refilled the coffee cups again. 'Thanks, Honey,' Dad said. 'You're real lucky, Mr MacTalfie. Working with human artists! I wish I could work with painters.'

'That's how I started,' Alfie said. 'I was a Visual Executive. I didn't like it.'

'How come?' I said.

'I had to transmit a picture into the artist's mind, and if I made a mistake, say I calibrated the colour wrong, it was a disaster.'

It turned out it was pretty much always a disaster. It turned out Alfie MacTalfie was colour blind.

Next, Alfie told us, he was transferred to the Music Section. He hummed tunes to composers while they slept, and the composers woke up ready to write the tunes. 'I had to leave that section too,' he said. 'It turns out I don't exactly have perfect pitch. Not exactly.'

He was in the literature section now, and it was his last chance.

'I deliver poems, short stories and picture books to artists. No novels. They take too long. That's one for the long-distance runner, if you get me. I'm more of a sprinter.' If there was one thing Alfie MacTalfie looked like, it was not a sprinter.

'The Art Department sounds brilliant,' Dad said.

'Come back with me and visit,' Alfie MacTalfie said. 'I'll show you around.'

'Hold it,' I said. 'How's that going to help with the APT? Dad only has two minutes left. We need to focus.'

'Oh, yeah,' Dad said glumly. 'We do.'

'Come back anyways,' Alfie MacTalfie said. 'Maybe you'll think of something there. Sometimes the best ideas come if you stop concentrating.'

This wasn't a reliable strategy. I mean, sure, if you stop thinking about a problem, an answer sometimes pops into your head. But not often.

'Let's do it,' Dad said. I sighed. Loudly. But

Dad's mind was made up. We were going to the Art Department.

We said goodbye to Honey and left, Dad trembling with the caffeine jitters. Alfie MacTalfie told us to meet him on the boardwalk at Venice Bridge, near the Art Department. He pressed his locate button and faded away, and me and Dad *whirr* **FIZZED** to Venice Bridge.

Chapter 25

The river was wide here, near the ocean. Boats churned through the water, or were docked, with stevedores loading and unloading the cargoes. (Stevedore is an uncommon word, but I know it because my full name is Stevedore Clipper.)

Alfie MacTalfie stood nearby on the steps of the grand, crumbling Art Department. We followed him in through immense oak doors. Inside, fidders swarmed up and down the great curved staircase, and yelled at each other across the lobby. It was utterly, superbly different from the Minute Minder Department.

We followed Alfie MacTalfie up flights of stairs, along corridors, through doors. It was like the higher you went, the more chaotic things became. By the sixth floor, fidders were bumping and blocking each

other, and papers stuck out of drawers, or lay in corners. Alfie's desk looked like a memory game: books, keys, coffee cups, banana, pens, scraps of paper, desk lamp, shoe.

'What a mess,' Dad said. 'Oh, my apologies.'

'It's a creative mess, is what it is. We Art Department Executives don't live by the rules, not like you Minute Minders.'

Everyone wants to be a maverick, I thought.

Dad opened a cupboard at random. 'This is where you keep the art ideas?' Sheaves of paper slid onto the floor. 'Oh, darn.'

'No problemo, that's all just reports and memos and stuff,' Alfie MacTalfie said. 'Come on, I'll show you the Hall of Ideas.' We abandoned the piles of paper on the floor, stepped over some spiral-bound reports, and followed Alfie MacTalfie again, up another flight of stairs and along a carpeted corridor. The din faded behind us, like we were in a ship sailing away from a storm. Alfie MacTalfie pushed open a high, carved door, and we entered a vast room, silent and orderly, with a thick, gold carpet and tall, stained-glass windows. The walls were lined with dark cabinets.

'This is the Hall of Ideas.' For the first time I heard something like respect in Alfie MacTalfie's voice. We stood a moment in silence.

I whispered, 'Where do the ideas actually come from?'

'Nobody knows,' Alfie MacTalfie whispered back.

'They arrive fully formed?'

'Yeah, but artists can change them. The ideas don't mind.'

Standing in this hall, I could almost hear the ideas breathing and whispering in the dark cabinets. I could almost see them glowing and gleaming, until the light I imagined inside the cabinets shimmered inside me. I added 'Art Department Executive' to my list of dream jobs.

On the far wall was a bronze plaque. I walked up to read it.

Ideas are the beginning.

Try them out.
Fail.
Try again.

To make ideas fly
All artists learn to try again.

'Is this true, what the plaque says?' I asked.

'Maybe.'

I read it again, and then once more.

'You know what, Dad? This could be the answer for Charlie. Remind him he's an artist, and that when an artist fails, they try again. Charlie could write that poem again, his own way. Good idea, right, Mr MacTalfie?'

'Stinky idea. Charlie Tobin's a kid. He won't understand about failing and trying again.'

'He's the same age as me, and I get it that if you give up when you fail, you probably stop yourself doing what you want.'

'It stinks.'

'You got anything better?'

He didn't. He looked mopily at Dad. Dad looked back, also mopily.

'What else can we do?' I said. 'Seeing as the original poem is... lost.'

'Are you saying it's my fault?' Alfie MacTalfie said.

Well, yes. He *had* covered the original poem with jam. On the other hand...

'You were right about visiting the Art Department, Mr MacTalfie,' I said. 'When we stopped concentrating on Charlie's poem, we found a plan.'

'And I guess this plan is all we got,' Dad said. 'On another note, hypothetically speaking, do you have vacancies here for failed Minute Minder Trainees?'

'Nope,' Alfie MacTalfie said. 'Especially not if I recommend them.'

Chapter 26

Over dinner, me and Dad discussed what to say to Charlie, and what voice to use. His football coach hadn't worked well.

'How about his teacher, Ms Carbury?' I said. 'Charlie likes her.'

'You're smart,' Dad said.

At 7.15 p.m., we were back on Charlie Tobin's shoulder.

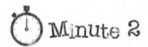 Minute 2

'Hey, Charlie,' Dad said. Charlie relaxed a little.

Ms Carbury's voice was a good pick. 'One lame poem, that's no reason to stop writing. Artists have to keep on trying, even if they fail. All artists experiment, and naturally they all make lousy art once in a while.

'You wrote one lousy poem, Charlie. That's the truth. But try again.'

Dad said Charlie could keep his poems just for himself, if he wanted. But he would feel better if he was writing poems. He could start by writing that Grey Fox poem again.

'And maybe leave out the bunny-wunnies,' Dad said.

Charlie listened. He didn't write. But I could tell that, in some part of him, he wanted to.

After we located home I visited Sandra May.

'Sandra May, if you fail at something, do you try again?'

'Of course! Everyone does, if it's important.'

'How about you try being friends with Charlie again?'

'How about you butt out of my business, Stevie?'

So I butted out, and we did some homework together.

'Stevie, how do I compare seven-ninths to three-eighths?'

We did a little mathematics.

'You're *imaginary*,' Sandra May thought. 'So how come I can do my sums better when you help? Is my imagination brain smarter than my maths brain?'

'Don't ask me,' I said. 'Hey, what does "euphoric" mean?'

'It means, like, jumping-around-dancing-happy.' She was good with words. I asked her what stymie meant and she knew.

'No wonder you and Charlie are friends. You both love words.'

'So much for you butting out.'

'Oops.'

Sandra May had to draw her family tree for homework, and I drew mine too.

Sandra May wrote her brothers' names: Ben, Cormac, Sam. I wrote 'Dicey'.

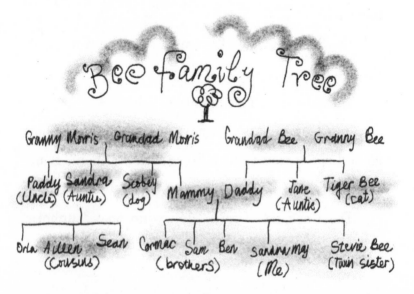

Bee family Tree

Granny Morris | Grandad Morris | Grandad Bee | Granny Bee

Paddy Sandra Scobey | Mammy Daddy | Jane Tiger Bee
(Uncle) (Auntie) (dog) | | (Auntie) (cat)

Orla Aileen Sean | Cormac Sam Ben | Sandra May | Stevie Bee
(Cousins) | (brothers) | (Me) | (Twin sister)

'I only have brothers,' Sandra May said. 'I would love a sister.'

'I have a sister,' I said, and I put in my twin sister's name. Annie. It felt strange to see her name beside mine, but it also felt like our names belonged together. Stevie and Annie.

I said, 'Hey Sandra May, we could be imaginary sisters. We could even be... twins.'

'Oh yeah!' she said, and she put my name right there, beside hers, on her family tree. Stevie Bee.

Next day, Friday 16 September, 7.44 p.m. We were with Charlie again. There was a lot riding on this minute: Dad's last chance to pass his test.

⏱ Minute 3

'*This lean, grey fox,*' Dad said.

Charlie heard Ms Carbury's voice.

He didn't go nuts.

'What is it about *this lean, grey fox?*' Dad said.

Charlie didn't do anything. We waited.

'Say something else,' I said.

'No need,' Dad said. 'Listen.'

I listened.

Charlie was repeating in his mind, '*This lean, grey fox*'. He heard the flutter of wings, and saw a grey fox slinking through the forest. He felt the shaking of small creatures, crouching away from the fox. A poem was taking shape.

After we left, Charlie wrote his own lean, grey fox poem. In his mind the fox was Badger, terrorising the forest creatures. Charlie imagined being a bird who could fly away and escape.

This lean grey fox
Shadows and stalks me,
But I swoop up,
Out of reach,
Gone.
You can't follow me, fox,
Or know where I fly.
Look, and look,
But I'm out of reach,
Gone.

Charlie wouldn't show his poem to anyone. No way. But writing it made him feel better, as though he had captured Badger on the page, while he, Charlie, escaped for a time. And he liked his poem. And he didn't care if nobody else liked it, and anyway they wouldn't see it.

Charlie Tobin was a poet again.

Chapter 27

Alfie MacTalfie's boss removed the 'FAIL' from his record.

Charlie was writing poems, so his life was a little better.

And Dad passed his Appropriate Practical Test.

It was a win-win situation, for Alfie, for the poem, for Charlie, for Dad. A win-win-win-win situation.

Dad was now a fully-fledged, officially licensed Minute Minder, and he didn't care who knew it. Okay, with all those rules and reports, Minute Mindering wasn't exactly his dream job. But it was a job. That was good enough, right?

I really hoped that was good enough.

The following Monday Miss Trent gave Dad his new locator, the one for licensed Minute Minders.

'We can go anywhere with this!' I said.

'As long as it's on assignment,' Miss Trent said. 'You can't use your locator willy-nilly.' Oh, well. It was still better than the trainee locator.

'Dad's a licensed Minute Minder now,' I said. 'So what about our three weeks anywhere-in-the-world?'

Miss Trent nodded. '19th of October,' she said, 'you're booked on our Vacation Locator.'

Like Dad's brand-new Minute Minder locator, the Vacation Locator could bring you anywhere. But it wasn't programmed for assignments, just for vacations.

This was Monday 19th September. That meant ... thirty days to our vacation. Miss Trent said, 'Any idea where you'll go?'

'Mexico,' me and Dad said together. Obviously.

'Fine,' Miss Trent said. 'Of course, you *must* keep your noses clean until then, or Mexico is cancelled.'

'We can do that,' Dad said.

'I know you can,' Miss Trent said. She shook Dad vigorously by the hand. 'You did it, Clipper,' she said.

'Well done. Don't get sentimental, but I'll miss you both.' She blew her nose.

My heart faltered, and I realised I would miss working with Miss Trent, too.

Back home,
I made a chart
and stuck
it on
my wall,
to count
down the
days to
Mexico.

Then I visited Sandra May.

'Imagine you could vacation anywhere in the world,' I said to her. 'Where would you go?'

'Linbradan,' she said without skipping a beat.

'And who would you bring?' I asked, kind of hoping she would say, 'My twin sister, Stevie.'

'I don't know,' she said. But she imagined cycling

with Charlie along Linbradan River, and camping with him in the forest. Then she strayed into real memories of Charlie: doing their homework together, and cycling together in Beckett Park, and the tin cans that carried their thoughts and secrets to each other.

Those tin cans still hung outside. I guess neither of them wanted to be the one to finally cut that string.

Chapter 28

Now that Dad was qualified, he needed to prove himself in the Minute Minder Department. That made him nervous. Plus if anything went wrong we could say, 'Adios, Mexico'. That made him more nervous.

And when Dad was nervous he made mistakes.

CASE HC40P/Cree-Sean

Thursday 22 September, twenty-seven days to Mexico. Dad brought Sean Cree to visit his friend, Andy Baros, who lived in Esker Lane. I recognised Sean from

Sandra May's memories. He was in her class, a decent kid, although he barely noticed Charlie or Sandra May Bee.

Sean's mother brought him to the top of Esker Lane, and Dad made sure he reached Sandi's house safely.

Except Sean wasn't supposed to visit Sandi – he was supposed to visit Andy. Andy, Sandi. Dad mixed them up.

No worries, Sandi was in class with Sean too. She took her guitar, and she and Sean both went to Andy's, right across the road. Sandi and Andy played guitar and Sean made a kind of drum kit from some cardboard boxes, and they decided then and there to start a band, called the Pink Frogs.

'It worked out fine,' Dad said. 'Right?'

'Are you kidding, Dad?' I said. 'We just brought a human kid to the wrong house!'

CASE HC77K/Li-Cheng

Monday 26 September, twenty-three days to

Mexico. Dad told the Li family to go south instead of north, and they ended up sailing to Portugal instead of Orkney. That actually worked out pretty brilliant. They loved Portugal.

VITALLY IMPORTANT POINT
Embrace the surprises in your life.

Friday 7 October, twelve days to Mexico. Dad said 'right' instead of 'left', and John Moss chopped down the wrong tree. That was tragic. You can't fix a chopped down tree.

VITALLY IMPORTANT POINT
What can I say? Some mistakes you can't fix.

If somebody saw Dad make a mistake they reported him, and we'd go to admin to receive our reprimand from Bert Buckley, the Chief's new secretary. Bert Buckley had big, sweet, long-lashed eyes, like a baby elephant. And he was klutsy as an elephant. He banged into things, he broke things, he lost things, he mixed things up. He was not a dream secretary.

He never mixed up reprimands though.

Dad corrected trainee essays. He rearranged Miss Trent's files by date, instead of alphabetically. He polished the Chief's golf clubs.

Because somebody always sees.

CASE HC 37A/Jed-Jungle

Tuesday 10 October, nine days to Mexico.

One reprimand that sticks in my mind was with Jungle Jed, a retired Minute Minder. Dad had to deliver a follow-up report to him. It had been sent by mail three times already.

Maybe he had moved house.

Maybe he was dead.

Maybe a beetle ate his post.

Jungle Jed used to travel the world doing Emergency Minute Interventions, whatever they were. He lived way out of our zone, way out of anyone's zone, in the mountains, and he liked to tell stories. There wasn't much more information on him, because Jungle Jed wouldn't write reports.

I liked him already.

Jungle Jed was a fidder, so Dad and I were both allowed talk to him, and we weren't limited to a minute. In fact we were told to 'take as long as it takes'.

whirr FIZZ... locate.

A weather-beaten cabin sat surrounded by high trees. Dad rapped on the door. I inhaled cool, mushroomy air and gazed up into swathes of leaves, flickering and whispering in the sky. Everywhere twitched and shimmered with a peaceful, natural kind of life.

'Yeah?' A hairy head poked out from a window. I could only see about ten percent of the face, the rest was a jungle of sprouts and locks and tangles of grey hair. This was Jungle Jed all right.

'Sir, we've a form for you to fill in,' Dad said. 'From the Minute Minder Department, sir.'

'Are you kidding me?' Jungle Jed said.

'It won't take a minute, sir,' Dad said.

'It sure won't,' Jungle Jed said. 'Because it ain't happening. I'm never filling in another form in my life.'

A Minute Minder after our own hearts.

'Could we just come in for a minute?' Dad said.

'Nope.' Jungle Jed shoved a shotgun out the window. 'Get the heck off my property.'

'Uh-oh,' Dad said.

Not the soft assignment we'd expected.

I decided to tell the truth.

'Sir, I heard a lot about you, and I've been wanting to talk to you a long time.' Okay, maybe not the whole truth. 'How about I fill in the form, while you tell us some of your amazing stories?'

'Smart thinking, Stevie,' Dad murmured.

Jungle Jed looked at me for a minute. Or maybe he was turned away; with all that beard I couldn't be sure. 'Come the heck in, then, sonny,' he said, and his head disappeared back inside.

'I'm a girl, sir,' I said, but quietly. So what if he thought I was a boy?

Inside smelled piney, like our old Linbradan cabin. I felt right at home. We sat down, and I read out some questions from the form.

Do you need support?

Would you be willing to make a video for Trainee Minute Minders?

Do you suffer from any of these illnesses? And a list of about thirty illnesses, from tooth decay to cold feet.

'Just fill in No for everything,' Jungle Jed said, and he settled back in his rocking chair and started talking.

'I was a freelance Minute Minder,' he said. 'Contract, not regular payroll. They sent me to every corner of the planet. Emergencies only.' He filled a pipe, and chewed on the end without lighting it, and talked.

He told us about the time in Italy when he woke human parents, shouting, 'Go check on the kids, go check on the kids!' The parents practically sleepwalked to the kids' room, and got them out before anyone even smelled smoke. The house burned down. It was a miracle, the newspapers said, that nobody died.

There was the time in the Rockies when Jungle Jed told a mountaineer to stop climbing and go into a shack. The mountaineer went in, and immediately a blizzard came up, trapping him safely inside. For ten days he heated snow on a stove for water, and he cooked pasta. Then he was rescued. He said the worst thing was he would now hate pasta forever. 'Miracle Survival', the news headline ran.

Another time Jungle Jed went to a jungle village and persuaded the leader to bring her whole tribe onto higher ground, before the river broke its banks and flooded all their homes. Another miracle. That's when he got the name Jungle Jed. (I would have bet it was because of his hair.)

'How do you know this stuff is going to happen?' I said.

'Mainly S.I.S.,' he said. We looked dumb. 'Heck, you mean they still don't tell regulars about the Secret Information Services?' He chewed at his pipe a moment. 'I'll tell ya. Far as I'm concerned, y'all should know about S.I.S.'

This was a whole area of the fidder world we had never heard of. The S.I.S. have reporters and investigators. They follow and foretell weather, politics and world events, and supply information to fidder departments.

'How do we get in touch with them?' I said. 'We could use their information, right, Dad?'

Dad nodded. 'Sure could!'

'Forget it,' Jungle Jed said. 'You can't contact them. They contact you. They only deal with dangerous cases, and big international cases, and they mainly use freelancers.'

'Darn,' Dad said.

'Boy, I had fun.' Jungle Jed rocked happily in his 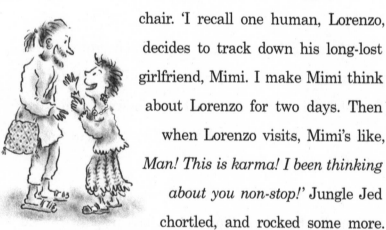 chair. 'I recall one human, Lorenzo, decides to track down his long-lost girlfriend, Mimi. I make Mimi think about Lorenzo for two days. Then when Lorenzo visits, Mimi's like, *Man! This is karma! I been thinking about you non-stop!*' Jungle Jed chortled, and rocked some more.

'Plenty times, humans never know how lucky they are. Like when I sent two brothers to cycle home by their Granny's, because if they went their usual way they'd probably be in a road accident. They never knew they were still alive because of me. And I tell ya, practically every week I froze the lights so some human wouldn't get hit by a car.' He turned to me. 'Even you could do that, kid. Input code 911X, point the locator at the lights, and holler, 'Freeze Red!'

I wrote the code down.

'Isn't that breaking rules, Mr Jed?' Dad said.

① Input code 911X
② Point locator at lights
③ Shout FREEZE RED

'Rules is good in their place,' Jungle Jed said. 'But I live my life the right way for me. And that usually works out right for my humans.'

I wrote that down too.

VITALLY IMPORTANT POINT
Live your own life the right way for you.

We sat there for hours, smelling the woody air, and listening to Jungle Jed's stories. He gave me hope that it was possible for a Minute Minder to have an exciting life.

'Come back any time, Hal Clipper,' he said when we were leaving. 'And bring your boy with you.'

Chapter 29

Work kept me busy, going everywhere with Dad, and keeping on top of all his paperwork and my schoolwork. I still visited Sandra May, but not every evening. I hardly ever saw Charlie, even in Sandra May's thoughts.

Dad, too, was working non-stop. It was worth it – he was up to date on his assignments *and* his reprimands. We were on track for Mexico.

Sunday 16 October, three days to Mexico. In admin, Bert gave Dad a memo.

'An Urgent Minute,' Dad said. 'Awesome!'

Urgent Minutes come out of the blue. They have no file, no background, no hassle. We love them.

MEMO URGENT MINUTE!!

Dad read the memo aloud. '*Lucia Cambra, waiting at airport; cousin Allegra to meet her; Allegra has incorrect date. Lucia speaks Catalan; can't ask for help. She's sixteen, satin-black hair, yellow backpack.*'

We located straightaway to the airport, and found Lucia outside Arrivals. I could feel her rising panic.

Dad selected 'Catalan' on the Translator.

'Take a breath, Lucia.'

Lucia looked startled... then tranquil.

'Everything will be fine,' Dad said.

Lucia gazed at the sky, tracking two little white clouds chugging across the blue.

'Bus 52 stops right by Allegra's,' Dad said.

Lucia was calm, but it was as though she couldn't hear Dad. She watched the clouds, like she had never seen these twists of white before. It was a puzzle.

Our minute ended. Lucia blinked, checked her map for Allegra's address, and saw bus-stop 52, across the road.

'It's like she's still in a trance,' I said. 'Gimme the locator, Dad.'

'Huh?'

I grabbed the locator from him and quickly tapped *911X*.

'Freeze red!' I zapped Jungle Jed's code at the traffic lights.

Pa-zang.

The lights flipped to red, just as Lucia stepped out – right into the path of a silver car. The car screeched to a stop. Lucia strolled across the road. I unfroze the lights and gave the locator back to Dad. The traffic started moving again.

Lucia smiled at the bus driver and pointed to the map. The driver helped her find the right coins for the journey, and the bus rolled away.

'She'll be fine,' Dad said.

The locator pinged. We were called to admin.

'Somebody must have seen me do Jungle Jed's traffic lights trick,' I said. 'Sorry I butted in, Dad.'

'Don't be,' Dad said. 'I'm proud of you. Maybe you saved Lucia's life.' He pressed a couple of locator buttons and we located to admin.

'The Chief wants to see you,' Bert said. Finally, we would meet the Chief. 'Don't worry. He's a bunny rabbit. His bark is worse than his bite.'

Me, I would be pretty scared of a barking bunny rabbit.

'Get in here NOW!' a voice yelled, and we scooted into the Chief's office.

The Chief was portly, practically circular, with a glossy, hairless head, and shining, winkle-picker

shoes. He was like Roly
Poly Wobbly Man, a toy
I had when I was little.
I felt like if I pushed
him over, he'd rock
right back up.

'Sit down, Clipper,'
he growled. He pointed
Dad to a shiny black
chair, then sat in the swivel chair at the other side
of his desk, and waved me to a pink velvet chair, by a
pretty fern in a terracotta pot.

'Nice fern,' I said.

'That was a gift from my grandmother, many
years ago,' the Chief said, in a fond voice. Then he
remembered himself. 'You're not here to talk
about the gosh-darn fern!' he
said, not in a fond voice. He
sat a moment, eyes closed,
breathing and counting.

'In: one two three four five,' he muttered. 'Out: five four three two one.' (Bert told us later this was a calming technique the Chief had learned – just after Dad joined the Minute Minders, coincidentally.)

A curtain sheltered the Chief's desk from the sun, which poured through the window onto Dad, practically blinding him. It was like in a movie, when someone shines a light in the victim's face to make them talk.

'I don't like working Sundays,' the Chief said. 'And I don't like rule-breakers. Tell me. What made you talk to Lucia Cambra in Cat?'

'Catalan,' me and Dad corrected him.

'Cat,' the Chief said. He pressed a button at the side of his desk. Blinds slid down the windows, and the lights dimmed. A video player started to hum, and we saw our time in Tassimity Airport projected onto a bare, white wall.

Humans aren't peaceful animals, especially in airports. In the video they rushed and pushed, dragging cases, running to gates, weighing luggage, checking tickets, scurrying, hurrying, worrying.

The camera zoomed in on Lucia, who was almost in tears. Then Dad talked to her, and she became calm as a summer lake.

And Dad was talking to her in Cat.

He had tapped 'Cat' instead of 'Catalan' on the Translator Language list.

We heard Dad say, 'Take a breath, Lucia'.

'Meeow-row,' Lucia heard. She was startled.

The Translator registered her agitation and recognised that it was to do with what Dad said. It instantly stopped transmitting his voice and played peaceful, meditative music instead. That's what Lucia heard. The music let her pause, until the minute ended.

In that minute of cloud watching, Lucia relaxed into dreamy thoughts. The Chief clicked 'translate'. The locator didn't decipher Catalan perfectly, but we got the idea.

Lucia thought, 'This a beautiful world is. I surmise everything be supreme. Maybe a tram or bus is for cousin. I bet peoples help. Peoples kind are.'

Then she blinked, checked her map, had a near escape from death and found bus 52. I was out of camera view when I pa-zanged the traffic lights, so for once nobody saw. Lucia got lucky, and so did I.

VITALLY IMPORTANT POINT
Ask your human to slow down, watch a cloud. And try it yourself. (Not in traffic.)

'You spoke to her in Cat!' the Chief said.

'Sorry, Chief,' Dad said.

'It was a mistake,' the Chief said. 'There will be a reprimand. But what I want to know, Clipper, is how come these things work out for you? I read your file, and nine times out of ten, your mistakes *work out*.'

'Just lucky, I guess,' Dad said.

'Smart,' I said. 'Dad's smart. Plus, he has

good instincts.'

'Instincts?' The Chief said
it like it was a rude word.
'It better not be instincts. It
better be something we can teach
the trainees.' He waited, and me and Dad thought
hard about how to help trainees make random errors.

'Heck!' the Chief said. 'You've made me late for, uh,
my next meeting.' He stood up. 'Any more mistakes,
and I might block your trip to Mexico.'

'But Dad got his licence, and he's up to date on his
reprimands,' I said. 'Isn't it the rule that we can go?'

'Maybe I changed the rule a little,' the Chief said.
He really didn't like working Sundays. He pointed at
Dad. 'I'm keeping an eye on you, Clipper. I'm not sure
I like how you operate. Most likely I don't. But I'm
keeping an eye on you.'

Then he gave us the reprimand, which was to
write about 'How to Turn Mistakes to Advantage'. He
ushered us out of his office and told Bert he had to go

to that 'other meeting'.

'Sure thing, sir,' Bert said. 'Your golf bag is waiting for you at reception.'

'Golf?' the Chief said. 'What can you mean?' and he rolled out the door.

We tried to write about making mistakes work out.

'The fact is,' Dad said, '*you* made this mistake work out, Stevie, with that freeze-the-light trick.'

'We can't write that,' I said. 'I was breaking a rule.'

The best we could come up with to Turn Mistakes to Advantage was 'just try something, and then try something else'. I was pretty sure that wouldn't make its way into any rulebook.

Chapter 30

Dad was reading his final assignment before Mexico.

'Wait,' he said. 'It's with a *cat*?'

Dad did not do well with cats. Cats pretty much ignored him. Or rather, they did the opposite of what he suggested. They did the opposite of what most fidders suggested. Me, I kind of admired them for that.

See, while cats are magical, mysterious and mischievous, they're also intelligent, inventive and independent. They have a 'can-do' attitude. They look after themselves, and don't need advice, thank you very much. It's when a *human* has a cat problem that a Minute Minder is called in.

Tuesday 18 October, one day to Mexico!

Fluffy was a gnarly, snarly bird-killer. Her human, Mr Macnamara, said the killing had to stop. Birds were feeding like crazy, and singing like opera stars, and generally looking awfully pretty in Mr Macnamara's garden. Mr Macnamara liked them. Sometimes he liked them more than he liked Fluffy. Which could end well for the birds, but very, very badly for Fluffy. Dad's job was to tell Fluffy to stop bumping off birds.

'What's the point of telling her that?' Dad said. 'She'll kill even more.'

He brooded.

'What about this?' I said. 'Tell Fluffy to kill *more* birds.' There was a moment's silence.

'By Jiminy,' Dad said. 'That's *brilliant*, Stevie.'

215

We located to Fluffy's home. She was in the garden, in the act of stalking a robin.

'Jump, Fluffy,' Dad said, using the translator. 'Catch that robin. Mr Macnamara is tired of all these shouty birds. You should work harder, and kill twenty birds a day for your human.'

'Twenty?' Fluffy snarled.

'Fifty,' Dad said. 'Kill fifty. Come on, you want to please your human, right?'

'Actually,' Fluffy said, 'wrong.' She sat and began cleaning her face. 'Let that Macnamara guy catch his own birds. I'm busy.' And she started playing with some yellow leaves that had fallen from Mr Macnamara's birch tree.

'Way to go!' Dad said to me, one-to-one, and he swung his arm around me in a shoulder hug. 'That was genius, Stevie!'

VITALLY IMPORTANT POINT

If you ask someone snarky to do the opposite of what you want, they might do what you want.

Back at headquarters we collected the Vacation Locator. Palm trees, white sand, pineapple shakes, here we come.

Then we heard, 'Hal Clipper to admin, please'.

My heart dipped.

In admin, Bert beamed at us like he had just won the Lottery, and said the Chief wanted to speak to us.

'Quit grinning like a squirrel,' Dad said, although I do not know that squirrels grin more than the rest of us. Anyway, Bert seemed unable to quit grinning like one.

BERT BUCKLEY

We went through to the Chief's office.

There were three things I liked about the Chief's office. Number one, it had the best view in the building. Number two, it had the pink-chair-pretty-fern corner. Number three – oh, there was no number three.

'Hey, Chief,' Dad said.

'Hey, Hal,' the Chief said. His voice was all shiny, like he was inviting Dad to a party. 'I got a special case for you.'

'Sure thing, Chief,' Dad said, very friendly. 'I can start in three weeks. Tomorrow, me and Stevie, we go to Mexico.'

'We'll send you a postcard,' I said, standing up.

'I hear you tried to have a cat kill birds,' the Chief said. His face had this innocent expression. I sat down again.

'We got a result,' I said. 'Fluffy won't ever kill another bird.'

'On paper, it's still a misdemeanour,' the Chief said. 'Technically I should report you to the Board.

It'd be a shame. You'd have to cancel Mexico.'

Oh, heck. The Minute Minder Board took an ice age to deal with a misdemeanour. I could feel Mexico slipping away.

The Chief extracted a file from the stack on his desk. 'You already know this kid,' he said. 'And I have to admit it's a difficult assignment. But you can do it, Clipper.'

VITALLY IMPORTANT POINT
If you're good at the difficult stuff
you get lumbered with the difficult stuff

The Chief flicked through the file. 'It will only delay you two days. Then you go to Mexico, I promise.' He placed a photo on the desk.

It showed a pale, worried-looking boy.

Charlie Tobin.

Chapter 31

'Bert will explain,' the Chief said. 'He volunteers with Charlie Tobin.'

'Bert Buckley?' I said. 'Your secretary Bert? That Bert?'

'Yeah,' the Chief said. 'That Bert. He *wants* to be a Minute Minder. I'm making him a trainee, and I'm making you his supervisor, Clipper.' The Chief looked to check the door was closed. 'See, I need Bert out of my hair. I need a proper secretary.'

That was understandable. But couldn't it wait three weeks?

'BERT!' the Chief yelled.

Bert stumbled in the door and grabbed the coat rack to steady himself. It toppled and knocked over the Chief's precious fern. Coats, hats, potting soil. It was a mess. The Chief did his counting-breathing thing.

'Hey, Hal,' Bert said to Dad.

'Sir,' Dad said. 'If I'm your supervisor, you call me sir.' Where the heck did Dad get that idea?

'Sorry. Sir.'

The Chief twirled on his swivel chair, and smiled, maybe because now he could have a proper secretary. I certainly had never seen him smile before. 'Sit,' he said, and me and Dad sat. Bert stayed standing, like that way he wouldn't do any more damage. I felt sorry for him.

But he had ruined our Mexico vacation.

Or to be more accurate, the Chief had ruined it.

Or to be completely, one hundred percent accurate, I had ruined it, with that 'Fluffy-kill-some-birds' stunt.

But who needs to be completely, one hundred percent accurate?

Bert started reading from a jotter.

'I volunteer with Charlie every morning at eight, when he's getting up for school. He's, like, in *despair*. He can't stand being bullied any more. He has no friends. And he's going to run away.'

'What?' Dad said. 'We have to prevent that. What's his plan?'

'He thinks he can stow away in a ship, like in a movie, and leave his problems behind.'

'Movies aren't real,' Dad said. Gee, thanks, Dad.

'No, sir.'

'Some people think they're real. But they're not.'

'Yes, sir.'

I thought about Charlie, vulnerable, abandoned by Sandra May, bullied and lonely...

'Charlie would be in big danger if he ran away,' I said. 'He's not streetwise.'

'Exactly,' the Chief said. 'Even streetwise

runaways are in danger. This is an emergency.'

'How do you know his plans, Rookie?' Dad said.

'See this poem?' Bert showed us a page with some writing. It started like this:

S5o 1x1z

'How is that a poem?' Dad said.

Bert explained that Charlie had developed a code to keep his poems private, and Bert had worked it out. Charlie replaced vowels with numbers: 'a' became '1', 'e' became '2' and so on. The other letters he switched up one, so 'b' became 'c', 'c' became 'd', right around the alphabet in a circle, until 'z' became 'a'.

'S5o 1x1z means run away,' Bert said. 'The rest of the poem describes being a stowaway and all that.'

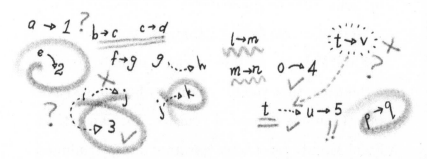

I was impressed. How had Bert deciphered Charlie's code? I pictured him studying it during his long office days, instead of filing assignments or making calls for the Chief.

'I gotta go in five,' the Chief said. Dad pretended not to hear. He enjoyed pretending not to hear the Chief. It was like a hobby.

'We'll go with you tomorrow for your volunteer minute, and take it from there,' Dad said to Bert. 'You, Rookie, have to do exactly what I say. Which will probably be to stay quiet and stay staying quiet.' He turned to the Chief. 'But I gotta get a Fluid Minute.'

'No way, Hal!' the Chief said. 'You know we can't do that. Fluid Minutes are for international situations. Politics and stuff.'

Well, of course we knew that.

Fluid Minutes are precious as diamonds. You can use them any time you like, with any human you like – more than one human, if you like. You can extend a Fluid Minute, so strictly speaking it isn't a minute, it's just – time. You can pause working with your human, and start again later the same day, or carry it over to the next day. Dad often said all minutes should be Fluid Minutes. But Fluid Minutes have a randomness that most Minute Minders dislike. Plus, they take about a month to write up.

'We only have two days,' Dad said. 'I need to be free to work with Charlie any time. The only way to do that is with a Fluid Minute. And we need a Monitor Tab.'

'I'll give you a Monitor Tab, Hal,' the Chief said. He stood up from his desk and went to the door. 'I'd like to give you a Fluid Minute too, I really would, but I can't.' He picked up his coat, shedding potting compost onto the carpet. 'However. I'm leaving the office now. If you come across a Fluid Minute Certificate hereabouts, for example in my right-hand bottom desk drawer, who's to say I would ever know?' He picked up his golf bag and opened the door. 'You might not know this,' he said, 'but Fluid Minute Certificates are orange.'

He left.

Dad whipped open the Chief's right-hand bottom desk drawer and pulled out an orange sheet of paper. Our Fluid Minute Certificate.

'You any good at forging the Chief's signature?' Dad asked Bert.

'It's one of my best things,' Bert said. 'If I say so myself.'

Bert was indeed an excellent forger, and he demonstrated his skill now.

CASE
HC39R/Tobin-Charlie

Chapter 32

Next morning, Wednesday.

CASE HC39R/Tobin-Charlie

We should have been in Mexico.

Instead, we were in Charlie Tobin's bedroom with Bert. First, Dad fixed a Monitor Tab to Charlie's ear, and programmed it. Now the locator would beep if Badger came close to Charlie, or if Charlie did something out of the ordinary, like hiding in the school boiler house, or skipping school.

Then we sat on Charlie's shoulder, waiting for Bert's minute.

I have to admit I'm kind of excited just before a Minute Minder comes onstage. It's like just before a movie starts. Like just before you open a new book. Probably like just before you press 'locate' on the Vacation Locator for Mexico.

Tap, tap. Charlie's mother's head appeared in the door. 'Rise and shine, Charlie,' she said. Charlie didn't move. She came over and kissed him on the top of his head. 'Come on, pet,' she said softly. Charlie still didn't move. His mother said, 'I'll make you some hot chocolate,' and she left.

Bert started his minute.

'Get up, Charlie, come on.' The voice he had copycatted was dramatic and arrogant.

'I can't,' Charlie thought. 'I'm sick.'

'You're not sick!' Bert said. 'Come on, Charlie. Look how this makes your mother feel! You know you're worrying her, right?' His voice was too loud. 'You think I didn't want to skip school sometimes? You think life is easy for the rest of us?' Charlie groaned and flopped over onto his front. 'Come on, Charlie! Forget those bullies, who needs friends?' Bert had lost it, but he didn't stop. 'Get up! Charlie, Charlie! You're hopeless! If you don't go to school, you won't get a job, you won't have a life! You want to ruin your life? Ruin your whole—' *Ping*.

Boy, was I glad *that* minute was over.

Bert looked at Dad. I looked at Dad. Dad looked at Bert.

Silence.

'But sir, he will ruin his whole life.'

'Let's go to the strategy station,' Dad said stiffly.

The strategy station was in the basement of Headquarters. We found an empty cockpit, put on headphones, and watched Bert's minute on screen. We saw Charlie in despair, and Bert jumping up and down and yelling. Dad turned the volume down.

'Who's your volunteer trainer, Bert?' he asked. Whoever it was should have trained Bert to be gentler with his human.

'Mr Sand.'

'Holy Jamoley,' I said. Mr Sand would have been a major in an army, if fidders had armies. 'Poor you.'

'Stevie,' Dad said. 'That's unprofessional.'

Sure, it was unprofessional, but hey. I'm a kid.

'Do you think I helped?' Bert asked.

'Yeah,' Dad said. 'Like a cat in a canary house, you helped. Like a bucket of sand in a desert, you helped. Like singing lessons for a frog, you helped.'

'I told him what my parents told me when I didn't want to go to school.' Bert sounded peeved. Dad did not appreciate peeved. 'It didn't do me any harm.'

'That's debatable,' Dad said. 'But in any case, you can't tell a kid he's hopeless. He'll believe you. Then he just can't change.'

Bert kept his peeved face intact. Dad muttered.

'Whose voice did you copycat?' I asked. Bert said it was Raven-man, Charlie's favourite superhero. Not a bad idea but...

'We'll try a different voice,' Dad said. 'It could embarrass Charlie to be reminded he can hardly get out of bed by someone who saves the planet every day before breakfast.'

Chapter 33

Our next step was to go to Beckett School for break time. We arrived early and sat on the cold yard wall to wait in the stinging wind.

'I hate being cold,' Dad said, beating his hands together to warm up. 'It puts me in a bad mood.'

'I told you to put on two sweaters,' I said. 'I put on two sweaters.'

'Well, aren't you just so smart.' He certainly was in a bad mood.

'Sit on a leaf,' I said. 'It's not so cold as the stone.' There were plenty of golden beech leaves around, and we each found one to sit on.

'Use your eyes for once,' Dad said
to Bert.

'Yes, sir.'

'I can't believe you shouted at Charlie.'

'No, sir.'

'You call yourself a Minute Minder.' (To be fair,
Bert didn't call himself a Minute Minder).

'Whose voice will you use, Dad?' I asked, to
change the subject. 'How about Ms Carbury? She
helped Charlie before, and she's already copycatted
into the locator.'

Dad said yeah, he'd use Ms Carbury.

The school bell rang for breaktime. Hundreds of
kids spilled into the yard. Lots of them started playing
running and skipping games to keep warm. Sandra
May Bee, in her pink raincoat and navy school shoes,
was last out the door, and she stood in a corner.

We located to Charlie's shoulder, where he leaned
on the yard wall, pretending to read a book.

Charlie stumbled, and I almost fell off his shoulder. Badger had barged into him as soon as the yard duty teacher was looking the other way.

'Hey!' Badger said. 'Say sorry for bashing into me.' Charlie said nothing. 'You hear me, Bunny-Boy?'

'Sorry, Badger,' Charlie said.

'Don't do it again,' Badger said, and he pushed past Charlie and walked away.

Dad started our Fluid Minute.

'You're a nicer kid than Badger any day, Charlie,' Dad said. Charlie heard Ms Carbury's voice, and felt a little reassured.

'That Badger is Charlie's problem,' I said to Bert. 'Right Dad?'

'Part of it for sure,' Dad said. 'You should have figured that out, Rookie. Understand?'

'Yes, sir,' Bert said.

'I doubt it,' Dad muttered.

'Really, sir,' Bert said. 'I know what it's like to get picked on. Sir.'

He sure did. Dad was picking on Bert like he was a ukulele. It wasn't Bert's fault he didn't know how to be a good Minute Minder. He hadn't been trained yet.

'Do you mean I'm picking on you, Rookie?' Dad said. 'I'm doing you a favour. You –' The bell rang for the end of breaktime. 'DARN IT!' Dad said. 'We can't help Charlie much during class. We have to wait until lunchtime now.' He glared at Bert like it was all his fault, and located us back to headquarters lobby.

'Chief's office,' Dad snapped, and turned and galloped upstairs. Me and Bert followed, up hundreds of steps to the top floor. Dad crashed through admin, into the Chief's office. The Chief barely had time to hide his golf club.

'This... *whoof*... isn't... working, Chief,' Dad said. He was out of puff. We all were. I don't know why we didn't use the lift. 'I can't work with a human and supervise a rookie at the same time.'

'Oh, really?' the Chief said, purple-faced. It wasn't easy, perfecting your golf swing in an office. He kicked a golf ball under his desk. 'It's not working, Clipper? Well. Let's just review your minute.' I guessed by his tone that he had seen us in action already.

The blinds came down, and the Chief started the video. It did not make for pleasant watching. We all saw Dad acting like a bully to Bert, in full technicolour.

'Nice, huh?' the Chief said. Dad didn't answer. But I knew he didn't like to see himself behave like that, any more than we did.

He faced Bert. 'Okay Rookie. I was mean. I'm sorry. I blame the cold.'

'Thank you, sir,' Bert said.

But the Chief wanted more. 'You blame the *cold*?'

'Okay!' Dad said. 'Okay. I was just plain mean. I apologise, no excuses.' He held out his hand, and Bert shook it.

The Chief was so happy his eyebrows almost twitched. Maybe he was thinking what I was thinking.

VITALLY IMPORTANT POINT
You can't help someone learn by being mean to them.

Chapter 34

We went back to Beckett School at lunchtime. Everyone had finished eating, and now most kids were charging about in a giant game of Capture the Flag. The Pink Frogs sat on the wall, practicing a new song. It wasn't much of a song, but they were enjoying themselves. Charlie was in a corner, trying to be invisible. Sandra May stood nearby, taking mouse-sips from her thermos of hot chocolate.

Dad, Bert and me sat on Charlie's shoulder.

'There are hundreds of kids in school, Charlie,'

Dad said. 'Some of them would love to be friends with you.'

Nothing.

'You could join that game of Capture the Flag,' Dad said. 'Or go listen to the Pink Frogs.'

Charlie looked up. I felt him gather his courage.

He started towards the Pink Frogs.

'Good for you, Charlie,' Dad said. 'This'll be great.'

However, just then Badger went up to Sandra May, and Charlie saw him knock her thermos so that it clattered to the ground. I felt the heat of hot chocolate splattering her legs.

'Oops!' Badger said. 'My bad, Twinkle-Toes.'

Charlie swerved towards them.

'Hold it, Charlie,' Dad said. 'The Pink Frogs is a better idea.' But Charlie knew what he wanted to do. He walked right up to Badger.

'You did that on purpose,' he said.

'Butt out, Bunny-Boy.'

Charlie picked up Sandra May's thermos and held it out to her. She glimpsed Badger's expression.

'Yeah, butt out, Charlie,' she muttered, a little shaky.

Charlie stalled. Then he put the thermos down and walked away.

'Charlie, that was really kind and brave,' Dad said.

'Kindness doesn't get anyone anywhere,' Charlie thought. 'At least soon I'll never have to see these kids again.' Dad kept talking, but Charlie wasn't listening. He was imagining himself stowing away, going someplace that doesn't exist, somewhere even friendlier and more hopeful than Linbradan.

The bell rang for class, and all the kids traipsed
back inside. We located to the strategy station and
watched the lunchtime footage.

'Badger's not the only problem,' Bert said,
pointing to Sandra May.

'Forget her,' Dad said. 'She won't help.'

'She was scared,' I said.

Dad sighed. 'Yeah, Badger would scare any kid.
But Charlie tried to stand by her, and she rejected
him. We need to find someone else to help him.'

'Wouldn't that make trouble for them?' Bert asked.

'It might,' Dad said. 'But humans don't spend their lives trying to stay out of trouble. Not like Minute Minders.'

We watched the footage again in slow motion. Nobody in the whole yard seemed to even notice Charlie.

The locator beeped.

'Monitor Tab,' Dad said, checking it. 'Charlie's writing in the park again.'

Sometimes Charlie sat in Beckett Park to write down a poem idea before it disappeared forever. That's what he was doing now. He hadn't noticed Badger behind him, but the Monitor Tab had.

'Let's go,' Dad said, and located us to Charlie's shoulder.

Charlie's left sneaker had a hole in it, and that's where this poem started. He wrote 'A Hole in My Shoe' in his notebook, like this:

It would be a poem about how you can fix a hole in a shoe, or a road, but it's hard to fix a hole in your life. Bert just had time to decipher the poem title for us when Badger snatched Charlie's notebook.

Charlie lunged for the notebook, Badger shoved him, and we were flipped into the air when Charlie fell. We swept back onto his shoulder and he picked himself up. Meanwhile Badger opened the notebook, smirking, but his smirk vanished when he saw the code. He pocketed the notebook. 'I'll figure it out, Bunny-Boy,' he said, and sauntered away.

'He won't figure it out,' Dad said to Charlie. 'Not Badger. Not in a million years.'

That helped, about one percent.

But really, things were worse than ever.

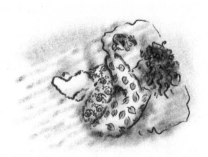

Chapter 35

That evening Dad was gloomy.

'Can we visit Sandra May?' I said. 'She had a bad day too.'

'I know, Stevie. But I can't help feeling disappointed in her. If you don't mind, I'll have an early night. You go visit her.'

So I located to Sandra May. She was scrooched on her bed, and I scrooched beside her.

'Hi, Sandra May,' I said.

'Hey, Stevie.'

I paused. I was about to start the kind of

conversation no friend likes, but real friends have, and sisters too.

'Why did you tell Charlie to butt out today?' I said. 'He was trying to help you.'

She scrooched tighter. 'He probably made things worse, butting in. What do you bet Badger's even meaner to me tomorrow?'

'Still, Charlie was brave.'

I stopped talking, like Dad did sometimes, to give Sandra May time to think for herself. And it was as though the silence allowed her to be with all her different feelings: anger, fear, loneliness, shame.

'I guess I'm just too scared to be a true friend,' she thought at me.

'I'd be really scared of Badger too,' I said.

Despondent, that's how we felt.

I changed the subject.

'Badger stole Charlie's notebook in the park,' I said.

Okay, not much of a change of subject.

'How do you know?'

'I was there. Charlie tried to get his notebook back.'

She contemplated friendship, and courage, and how Charlie stood up to Badger for her. Sandra May contemplating; that was a new skill.

The locator beeped. *Charlie Alert*. I clicked on Charlie's monitor information. He was sneaking out of home.

'Oh, no,' I said. Charlie had a backpack. It looked like he was running away a day early.

'What?'

'Charlie's going out – he's getting his bike.'

'At night?'

'Yes.'

'How do you know, Stevie?'

'It's like – I got a text. Heck. I better go tell Dad.'

'Wait! Where's Charlie going?'

I felt into Charlie's mind.

'He's running away. But...' I concentrated. 'First he's going to Badger's, to get his notebook back.'

'This time, I'm going to help.' Sandra May jumped

off her bed and pulled a sweater on over her pyjamas.

'No, you don't!' I said. Night in a big city was not the time for Sandra May to help Charlie.

'Yes, I do.' She squashed her fluffy pink bed socks into her twinkly sandals. 'I'm done with being too scared to be a friend.'

'You can't go out at night.'

'Watch me.' She put her pink rain jacket on over her sweater, and checked she had her keys. 'Don't come if you don't want.'

'Plus, why would you believe me?' I said. 'I'm imaginary.'

She put on her sparkly bike helmet.

'Well, I do believe you.' She went out her bedroom door. 'You always know stuff, Stevie.'

'Wait until tomorrow,' I said.

'Maybe I won't feel brave enough tomorrow,' Sandra May thought back. She was at the front door. 'Maybe I won't get another chance to help.'

Humans are stubborn. Sometimes even their terrible ideas won't shift. I might as well have shouted, 'Let's go, Sandra May! You and me, two ten-year-olds out at night in a dangerous city!'

She crept out of the front door, along the corridor, and pushed the button for the lift.

Should I locate home and tell Dad? Or should I stick with Sandra May, to help her stay safe?

The lift door opened and Sandra May went in.

'Do Right by Your Human,' I thought. I swooped onto her shoulder. 'And do right by your friend.'

The lift sped us downstairs. The instant it opened Sandra May dashed out, heaved open the front door and sprinted around to the back of Delvin Tower. She unlocked her bike and jumped on. Something in me was glad to see her

old, impulsive self again. In no time she was cycling hard along Lennox Street. She made a left onto Esker Avenue, where the trees of Beckett Park arched darkly over us. The city felt mysteriously empty. At a broken streetlight two homeless humans stood up when Sandra May cycled by.

'You go right home, girleen, d'you hear me?' one of them hollered.

'It isn't safe out!' the other called.

Sandra May cycled on, left again onto O'Malley Street, and now we could see Tip Top Bakes where Badger lived. A striped awning sheltered the bakery window. Above the awning a 'Tip Top Bakes' sign flashed orange, making the bare branches of a cherry tree outside seem to quiver.

And there was Charlie underneath the tree, holding his bike, looking up to where Badger's family lived over the bakery.

Sandra May's bike coasted silently to a stop. 'Charlie!' she whispered. He whirled around and looked at her bug-eyed.

'What are you doing here?' he asked.

'I want to finally be a proper friend,' she said. 'I want to help. That's if you'll let me.'

Chapter 36

Charlie stared at Sandra May. 'I don't need your help,' he said. He patted the tree. 'Badger took *my* notebook. *I'm* getting it back. You can go home.'

But Sandra May's old spirit was back. She wasn't going anywhere.

'I've seen Badger look out that window,' she whispered, pointing up. 'I bet that's his room.'

'Go away. It's nothing to do with you.'

'I'm staying, okay?'

Charlie didn't answer. He started to climb. Me and Sandra May watched. He put his left hand up, his right foot up, the other foot... which way? He was not a natural climber.

'Come down,' Sandra May whispered. 'I'll climb. You watch the bikes.'

Charlie muddled his way down. 'Okay,' he said. 'But this doesn't mean we're friends.'

Sandra May sprang onto the lowest branch and swung herself up like an acrobat, with me on her shoulder. She climbed higher, then shuffled along narrower branches to Badger's bedroom window. It was locked shut.

Sandra May looked down at Charlie. She spread her arms out and closed them together, and he understood she meant the window was locked. For a moment neither of them did anything.

'Meow,' called Charlie in a thin voice. I saw his thought: 'Pretend Badger's cat wants in.' I started to tell Sandra May, but she understood Charlie's idea without my help. She gave him a thumbs-up, and shimmied to the side of the flashing sign, so if Badger looked out he wouldn't see her. Charlie wheeled the bikes under the awning, out of sight. Then he yowled.

'MiAOOOw-ow-ow.'

Before long Badger came to the window and unlatched it.

'Pushkin? Kitty-kitty!'

Pushkin did not appear, and Badger locked the window again and went back to bed.

'Ree-ow-meow-meow. Meeeeeeuw.'

Badger opened the window again, and peered down to the street, called Pushkin, grumbled, locked the window and stomped back to his bed.

'Mi-OOOOW-ow-ow.'

The window opened. 'Pushkin!' Badger hissed.

He waited. 'I'm flippin' exhausted.'

He went back to bed, but this time he left the window ajar for Pushkin. He was nicer to his cat than he was to his classmates. The chilly night air waltzed in, and Badger burrowed deep under his duvet.

Sandra May inched onto the windowsill.

'Wait,' I said. 'He's not asleep yet.'

In a few minutes, Badger started to snore.

'Now,' I said.

Sandra May peered around Badger's bedroom, until her eyes found his schoolbag in the flashing orange light. Silently, she pushed the window wider, and slipped inside. I almost said, 'Be careful,' but she was already being careful. She crept over to where Badger's schoolbag flopped on the floor beside a table. Badger groaned and rolled over. Sandra May froze. He grumbled into sleep again. She slipped her hand into his schoolbag and fumbled around. Charlie's notebook wasn't there.

'On the table,' I said. She looked, and saw the

notebook appearing and disappearing in the orange flashes.

'See, you always know stuff, Stevie.' She pushed Charlie's notebook inside her jacket, stole back across the room, and hoisted herself onto the windowsill. Her left sandal snagged on a chair and clopped to the floor. She jumped back inside to fetch it.

Badger's eyes snapped open, and he bolted upright.

'*Twinkle*-Toes?'

'Evening, Badger,' Sandra May said. She grabbed her sandal and swung herself out the window and down the tree.

Charlie held the bikes, ready to get gone. Sandra May handed Charlie his notebook, and they high-fived each other.

'*Bunny*-Boy?' Badger was leaning out the window.

Charlie gave Badger a salute, Sandra May pulled her sandal on, and they cycled away together, both of them fizzing with happiness.

'The Three Musketeers,' I said.

'The Three Musketeers!' Sandra May yelled.

'Three?' Charlie shouted. 'It only took Two Musketeers!'

They cycled on, back to Delvin Tower, and dismounted.

'That was great,' Charlie said. 'You're a hero.'

Sandra May looked down at her pyjama bottoms and fluffy socks. 'Some hero,' she said, grinning.

'Ask him not to run away, Sandra May,' I said.

'After how I treated him,' she thought, 'I can't ask him *anything*.'

'Yes you can.'

So Sandra May spoke. 'Charlie, please don't skip school tomorrow. I'll need your help. Badger will be mad as a goat.' They looked at each other a moment.

I held my breath.

'Okay,' Charlie said. 'Just tomorrow.'

They locked their bikes and made their way back into Delvin Tower. They took the lift to floor 9, and whispered goodbye to each other when Charlie stepped out. The lift doors closed again.

'Sandra May, that was amazing,' I said.

'We really were three Musketeers, Stevie,' Sandra May thought. 'You're the third Musketeer. But Charlie wouldn't understand. I'm keeping you to myself.'

Chapter 37

I slept late next morning, and I was tired when Dad called me.

'I'm coming!' I jumped up, still in yesterday's clothes, and ran to grab Dad's hand. We located to Charlie's bedroom, where Bert was already waiting.

Time to explain about last night.

'Dad,' I started. He held up a hand.

'Later, Stevie, please. Charlie plans to run away today. We need inspiration, not distraction.'

Thanks for the get-out clause, Dad.

'I'm starving, Mam,' Charlie said in the kitchen.

'Good!' she said. Charlie ate a huge bowl of porridge with raisins.

'He seems... happy,' Dad said. We could all feel it.

'Is that because he's running away?' Bert asked. 'That's bad.' We felt into Charlie's thoughts. He was remembering last night, in drifty, sleepy fragments, all out of sequence.

Badger looking down from the window saying, '*Bunny*-Boy?' in that bewildered voice.

Charlie going, 'Miaow'.

Sandra May leaping up the tree like a gymnast.

'Is he remembering a dream?' Bert said.

'I guess,' Dad said. 'And it's a happy dream.'

Charlie left to catch the bus to school. He was still smiling inside.

'He really *does* seem okay,' Bert said. Dad nodded.

On the bus Charlie read a Raven-man comic, and in class he sat alone as usual. Then Sandra May arrived and sat beside him. They grinned at each other.

'What the...?' Bert said.

Dad felt into Charlie's thoughts. 'How did this happen?' he said. 'It's like they're friends again.'

'Maybe that wasn't a dream?' Bert said.

'We'll figure it out later,' Dad said. 'Right now, we have to stop Charlie running away.'

'I don't think he will,' I said.

'You could be right,' Dad said.

Ms Carbury arrived, and class started. Badger glowered at Sandra May and Charlie from the other side of the room. I felt into Badger's mind. It was spiky and hot, full of anger. I got out of there pretty quick.

 Dad concentrated on Charlie, but there were no thoughts about stowing away on a ship.

'I'm going to talk to him, Bert,'

Dad said, 'and see if I can find out more.'

'Yes, sir.'

Dad whispered to Charlie, 'Looks like you're friends with Sandra May again.' Charlie looked at Sandra May and smiled.

'Could be,' Charlie thought back.

'That's good,' Dad said to Bert. 'And he's not thinking about running away.'

'Should you keep talking to him?' Bert asked.

'Sometimes we step away,' Dad said. 'Then the human has a chance to let things settle.'

'So we'll just watch his thoughts for now?' Bert said.

Dad nodded. 'Until break time. That'll tell us a lot.'

When the bell rang for breaktime everyone erupted into loud talk and bundled out of the classroom. Me, Dad and Bert stayed on Charlie's shoulder, and Charlie and Sandra May ran together down the corridor, into the chilly yard.

Badger pushed right up to them in front of all their classmates. 'You two,' he snarled. He turned to the others. 'They broke into my home last night!'

'Slap on the handcuffs,' Sandra May said, holding out her arms. I could feel her bubbling with life inside, just like the first time I met her, chopping up her bedspread in Linbradan.

Badger noticed the yard teacher drifting towards them. 'This isn't over,' he whispered at Charlie and Sandra May, and he slunk off.

It wasn't over. But for now, Charlie and Sandra May didn't care.

The teacher stopped to help a little kid tie her shoelaces.

'Did you actually break into Badger's?' Sean Cree asked Charlie.

Charlie grinned. 'He stole my notebook,' he said.

Sandra May and Charlie described what had happened last night, every step of the way.

'Wow,' Andy Baros said. Sean Cree clapped Sandra May on the back.

'Were you not scared?' Sandi asked Charlie.

'I wanted my notebook back.'

'And I wanted to help Charlie,' Sandra May said. 'He's my best friend.'

'Good for you!' Andy Baros said, and he high-fived Charlie and Sandra May, one hand each.

I floated from Charlie's shoulder to Sandra May's.

'Sandra May, that was brilliant,' I whispered.

'Yeah, Stevie,' she thought back. 'It was ace.' She nudged Charlie. 'Nice work, pal,' she said.

Charlie nudged her back. 'You and me both,' he said.

I felt a nip of sadness, and wished for a moment that the three of us could be friends.

Then I sailed back to Dad and Bert. We located to the yard wall, and watched. Even from this distance, I could hear Charlie and Sandra May laughing together, friends again.

Chapter 38

Charlie's case had only taken a couple of days, and now, at last, we could go to Mexico.

Except there was a fly in the ointment. A tiresome, troublesome, tricky fly. A fly called the Chief.

Me and Dad were called to his office. Perry Eriksson, the Chief's new secretary, stopped click-clicking on his computer and said, 'There's been a complaint.'

'Who complained?' Dad said.

'I complained,' the Chief roared from his office. 'Get the heck in here, Clipper.'

Oh, brother.

We went in.

'I watched this morning's video,' the Chief yelled, before we even closed the door. 'Clipper, you blew it. This time your job is on the line.'

'I don't know what you mean, Chief,' Dad said. 'Like, I really don't know what you mean.'

'I couldn't believe what I saw,' the Chief said. He narrowed his eyes at Dad. 'Are you listening, Clipper? You don't look like you're listening.'

'Sure, I'm listening, Chief.' Dad never looked like he was listening.

'Are you worried? You don't look one bit worried.'

'Sure, I'm worried, Chief,' Dad said.

But I could tell he wasn't really worried. He was too happy about Bert and Charlie and Sandra May Bee to worry. And how could Dad worry when we were going to Mexico?

The Chief took off his navy jacket. His bald head was slick with sweat. The Chief was harassed, and that made him too warm, even in October.

'Three times I looked at your video,' the Chief said. 'I looked real close.'

Dad shook his head, as though to say, 'You have a tough job, Chief.'

'Nobody else has seen it. I don't want them to.'

A look of uneasiness crept over Dad's face. I started to feel something like concern too.

'Of all the things I thought you'd do, Clipper,' the Chief continued, 'I never thought you'd let Stevie talk to a human.'

It took a moment for the Chief's words to sink in. Dad looked stunned. I was worried now, good and proper.

'Stevie – what?' Dad said. 'She talked to a human? But – she isn't trained. A human couldn't understand her.'

The Chief played the video back.

There I was, whispering, 'Sandra May, that was brilliant.'

There was Sandra May, thinking, 'Yeah, Stevie, it was ace.'

'Sounds like she understood Stevie LOUD and CLEAR,' the Chief said. 'She used Stevie's gosh-darned name! What the heck is happening, Halyard Clipper? You let your kid get to know a human, first name terms? What are they – *friends*?'

'Dad didn't know,' I whispered.

'Be quiet,' Dad said.

The Chief kicked his desk, rubbed his patent-leather-toe on the back of his trousers, snarled around the office, and yelled at the door. After what seemed like hours he cooled down by about one degree and sat behind his desk. His set jaw said, 'I'm not disappointed. I'm angry.'

'This is serious, Clipper,' he said. 'What if humans found out about us because of Stevie? It could ruin everything! Humans wouldn't know whether or not to take our advice. They might think we're trying to trick them. They might think, you know...'

'We're fairies,' I said. He ignored me, luckily. This was not a time to make myself heard.

The Chief rolled his chair back from his desk, closed his eyes, and did his breathing exercise. In: one two three four five. Out: five four three two one. His hands lay palms upwards on the broad knees of his navy trousers.

Me making friends with a human, that was enough to put the Chief off his golf stroke.

It was enough for Dad to lose his job.

Maybe it was enough for Dad never to trust me again.

In: one two three four five. Out: five four three two one.

The Chief opened his eyes and saw us, and clearly did not enjoy the scenery.

'Go,' he said. 'If I had my way, I wouldn't ever see you again. But at least go the heck away until tomorrow.'

Dad was silent until he had located us home.

Then he was thunderous.

'After all we said, you spoke to a human? How long has this been going on?'

'A while.'

'I can't believe you lied to me like that.'

'I didn't lie, I promised not to read your books and I didn't...'

'You knew you were deceiving me, right?'

'Well...'

'At least tell the truth now!'

'Yes.'

'This has lost me my job, probably.'

'I'm sorry, Dad. I'll stop.'

'Too right, you'll stop.'

Dinner was gloomy. But afterwards Dad listened enough for me to explain that Sandra May didn't know about fidders,

271

and that she thought I was her imaginary twin sister. Dad's face softened.

'So she's your imaginary twin sister too?' he said.

I nodded. 'But I don't think she wants to be any more. Now that she and Charlie are friends again.'

Dad put his arms around me and we were both quiet for a minute. Maybe longer.

'Dad, what are we going to do?' I said.

'We'll do what we always do, Stevie,' Dad said. 'We'll try something, and then try something else.'

Chapter 39

Miss Trent joined us in the Chief's office next morning. She didn't smile, but I was glad she was there.

I explained that Sandra May thought I was her imaginary twin sister, and the Chief said he hoped that was true. Then he said to listen up, and listen good.

'I'm suspending you for a month, Clipper,' he said. 'If it wasn't for Miss Trent, I'd fire you.'

Dad still had a job. I felt wobbly with relief. Miss Trent really was something.

'Miss Trent heard about what happened yesterday,' the Chief continued. 'She suggested a humdinger of a reprimand.'

Despite my relief, I felt tired. At this moment, it seemed a Minute Minder's life was one long chain of catch-up. You made a mistake, and you were given a reprimand assignment. You made a mistake with the reprimand assignment, and you got another reprimand assignment. You made a human friend and you were suspended for a month, *and* reprimanded.

'Tell them, Miss Trent,' the Chief said.

'Here's my idea,' Miss Trent said. 'The Minute Minder Department needs a handbook for rookies, to address our staff shortages and help with recruitment. You'll write it, Hal, based on your experiences and Stevie's extremely useful VIP journal.'

'Writing the handbook is your reprimand, Clipper,' the Chief said. 'Afterwards, Stevie goes to boarding school, and you keep your job.' He sneaked a peep to see how Dad was taking this. 'I'm mad at you, Clipper, but I don't want to lose you. I think I don't anyway.'

'Sure you don't, Chief,' Dad said. 'Of course you don't. But give me a different reprimand. Give me ten. I can't write a book, Chief. I'm not so hot with words.'

'You're the best person for the job, Clipper,' Miss Trent said.

I could see why she picked Dad. He was probably the only Minute Minder in the world with the flair to write this handbook.

Dad – or me.

'Maybe you're not like other Minute Minders,' the Chief said. 'Maybe not always playing by the rules. You got your own ways. Heck, you're... you're *individual*.' He said that like 'individual' wasn't an insult in the Minute Minder Department.

Dad said, 'I really couldn't write that book.'

The Chief said, 'Yes, you could.'

'Couldn't.'

'Could.'

'Couldn't.'

'Maybe you could, Dad,' I said. ('Or maybe I could,' I thought.)

I gave the Chief my kindly smile.

Why did I give the Chief my kindly smile?

Because I was starting to have an idea, is why. What if I could transform this handbook into our get-out-of-jail-free card?

'What would Dad have to write?' I said.

'Mainly about some of his cases,' Miss Trent said.

'He needs to write them up anyways,' the Chief said.

Yes, Dad had a huge backlog of reports to do. That was my fault. I had promised to keep his reports up to date as part of my schooling.

The thing was, I forgot. And by 'forgot', I mean 'couldn't be bothered'.

'This way,' the Chief continued, like he had read my mind, 'you don't have to catch up on your dad's paperwork, Stevie kid. The handbook would be instead of that, written whatever way he likes.'

'Within reason,' Miss Trent said. Caution is the name of the Minute Minder game.

'Sure, within reason,' the Chief said. He gave us a list of things we'd have to include in the handbook, from explaining Minute Minder assignments, and schedules, to describing different kinds of minutes: Urgent Minutes, Observation Minutes, Fluid Minutes and so on.

Dad looked puzzled. He could see I thought we should write this darned handbook, but he couldn't for the life of him figure out why.

Maybe so you don't lose your job, Dad.

Maybe to make up to you for being friends with a human.

'Well, Stevie?' he said. He was letting me take the lead. Despite everything, he wanted to trust me again. The Chief didn't go so far as to smile, but his eyebrows lost their grip on each other.

'If Dad agrees,' I said, 'does he write the handbook here, in headquarters?'

'Heck, no way,' the Chief said. 'He's suspended. Write in your apartment, or the park, wherever.'

Wherever...

We still had the Vacation Locator at home, poised for Mexico. Miss Trent looked like she knew what I was thinking, and she finally smiled at me.

Me and Dad stood to leave.

'Remember, make us sound *enticing*.'

'Yes sir, Chief,' I said. I'd look that word up later. 'Thanks, Miss Trent. Thanks, Chief.'

'Okey dokey,' the Chief said.

Mission accomplished, he was thinking.

And so was I.

'Yeah, Chief,' I said. 'Okey, as you say, dokey.'

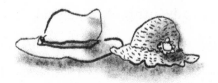

Chapter 40

Zoom forward one day.

Mexico.

Finally.

I was on the beach, in a hammock, under a palm tree. Dad was swimming in the wide blue ocean; his third swim of the day. Some human kids were splashing and yelling in the water. They weren't even bugging me. The sun was tickling my toes. My creative juices were flowing.

I was writing the truth about the Minute Minder Department. Not exactly what the

 Chief had asked for, but exactly what the department needed. The adventurous fidder kids, the ones with gigantic hearts, the ones who knew what it was like not to belong, lots of them would read this handbook, and sign up to be Minute Minders. And that would be good for everyone.

Every evening me and Dad had dinner in a beach shack called La Playa, with our toes in the sand, discussing everything under the sun.

We talked about the humans we knew – the poets and adventurers, the teachers and musicians, the kids. We talked about the fidders too – the office workers and farmers, the Listeners and Art Executives, and the ones who lived courageous lives, like Jungle Jed. We talked, me and Dad, about what kind of lives *we* wanted to live.

 It took me two weeks to write the handbook. Finally one evening I wrote *The End.*

I read the last page again.

That's what a Minute Minder's life is like. You work with humans to make their lives better, you work to let your Chief play golf in his office, and do you even have a vacation? Not likely.

So why be a Minute Minder?

Because it's important work. Because it helps humans and cats and dogs. Because somebody has to do it – somebody caring, and daring, and patient.

Why not you?

The sinking sun coloured the sky mango and pineapple. I stretched my arms and wiggled my shoulders. You get stiff even in a hammock. 'Do you want to read it, Dad? It's supposed to be your book.'

'Naw,' Dad said, in his sleepy Mexico voice. 'I trust you, Stevie. I bet you wrote it perfect.'

'It tells the truth, though,' I said. 'That's not exactly what the Chief asked for.'

'But it's what he wants,' Dad said. 'Everyone wants the truth.'

I hoped he was right.

'Okay. I'll send it now.'

I wrote an email to the Chief.

Dear Chief,

I hope this finds you well. Dad and I are working hard. Please find attached the Minute Minder Handbook.

Yours sincerely,

Stevedore Clipper

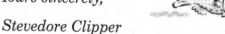

I attached the document and pressed send.

Then I switched off the computer. Dad fetched two tinkling glasses of papaya and lime juice. He raised his glass. 'To the handbook.'

'The handbook,' I answered, and we clinked glasses.

We borrowed snorkelling masks, and boy, you should see those fish. We played beach volleyball with other fidders. Juanita Esperanza, whose parents owned La Playa, taught me how to play the marimba.

We sat on a seashell at sundown and watched the sun sinking behind the ocean. And the next day was the same, and the one after that, and the one after that.

How come everyone doesn't come and live in Mexico?

Chapter 41

Then it was over. We located back to chilly, damp Tassimity. The city honked and whooped, brimming with life. It felt good.

Our suntanned feet had barely hit the ground when we were called to the Chief's office.

The office hadn't changed. The Chief hadn't changed. Maybe his face was a richer purple. He didn't say hello. He didn't admire my Mexican necklace.

Dad moved the black chair out of the sharp wintry sunlight, hitched up his shorts and sat. I pulled the pink velvet chair over to sit by him.

'We're not publishing your handbook,' the Chief said, and he started making a list, counting on his fingers. 'You say we have too many rules, and too much paperwork. You say it's okay to make mistakes sometimes. You say I play golf on departmental time.'

'But it's all *true*,' I said. I felt unexpectedly sad for my book.

'Hal,' the Chief said, looking at Dad. 'You got to rewrite it! You didn't even put the top ten rules in!'

'We're not changing a word,' Dad said. 'Not a single word.' He reached out and gripped my hand. He hadn't read the handbook, but he trusted me.

'May I remind you,' the Chief said, 'your job is on the line.'

Dad didn't need reminding.

Nor did I.

We wanted the Chief to publish our book, but if he wouldn't, we had a Plan B.

'Sorry Chief,' Dad said.

'Dad quits,' I said.

'He can't quit,' the Chief yelled. 'He's fired!'

It didn't matter if Dad was fired or if he quit. Either way, we were leaving the Minute Minder Department. Either way, Dad wouldn't get another job in any fidder department. Either way, this was a good day.

Maybe our Plan B was crazy. Or maybe some of what Dad had been telling the humans had rubbed off on us. Why shouldn't we follow our dreams, too?

Me and Dad, we located home. It was still morning, and we wanted to finalise details for Plan B.

Right away I started making changes to *The Minder Minder Handbook*. I deleted boring bits, and wrote more about our personal experiences, and I changed the title.

Dad called Alfie MacTalfie, and we met in Honey's Diner. After Alfie had eaten enough food to supply a school picnic, Dad told him we had a proposal.

'Minute Minders don't get to have proposals,' Alfie MacTalfie said.

'I'm not a Minute Minder any more,' Dad said.

'I quit.' Alfie gaped, losing a substantial portion of blueberry muffin from his mouth. 'And in the interests of full disclosure,' Dad said, 'I was also fired.' There was a pause while Alfie rearranged his view of Dad.

'What you gonna do now, Hal?' Alfie asked. There was concern in his voice, like we were friends. I guess we were.

'Dad's going freelance,' I said. 'Like a Private Eye.

He'll take on the tricky jobs nobody else can handle. But instead of being chewed out for thinking outside the box, he will get major thanks from his grateful clients.'

Alfie wobbled his head to mean, 'Maybe yes, maybe no'.

'Before that, though,' I said. 'We have a book that wants writing. You got a human author to spare?'

'You're kidding!' Alfie MacTalfie said. 'I'm way behind in my assignments already.'

Just what I hoped to hear.

'*We'll* deliver the book,' I said. 'No strings.'

'That's a pretty cute deal,' Honey called over the counter.

'Boy, Honey,' I said. 'You got good ears.' I lowered my voice, and Alfie MacTalfie leaned forward to hear.

'You give us a writer's name,' I said. 'Dad gives them the book. Pick someone you don't want to work with.'

I could see Alfie searching for a flaw in the plan. I could find about ten, but he couldn't find any.

'It's a perfect plan,' I said. Liar, liar, pants on fire.

Alfie smiled. Dad smiled. I smiled. Honey smiled. She really did have very good ears.

Alfie could be in trouble if he was found out, but he couldn't resist losing a tricky writer.

'I'll do it,' he said.

VITALLY IMPORTANT POINT
Sometimes it's worth breaking rules.

Chapter 42

Alfie called to our apartment that evening and handed Dad a file.

Mary Murphy, Children's Author, Inishnaroon, Galway.

'She's not in Tassimity?' Dad said.

'That's how the Art Department rolls. We travel lots of places.' Another reason to bump 'Art Executive' to the top of my career list.

Mary Murphy hadn't written anything for ages, and she had no fresh ideas. Mainly she and her dogs just hung out in their cottage, or rambled around the island of Inishnaroon.

'She sounds lazy,' Dad said. 'Is she all you got?'

'Yep,' said Alfie. 'What's that smell?'

'Chilli potatoes.'

Mary Murphy's home was messy, according to the file. I guessed she was easy-going. Good. Easy-going humans are pushovers.

The phone rang, and Dad picked up. 'Hi Perry... Yeah, I know.' Dad scribbled on a scrap of paper. Perry made earnest noises on his end of the phone-line. 'Say that again, Perry?' Dad scribbled some more then said, 'I'll call you tomorrow.' He hung up. 'We have a problem. There's a clause in my contract.' He read his notes. 'For the month following a licence being revoked, the ex-Minute Minder is required to be available to assist in finalising any such assignments as the department deems in need of clarification.'

'What's that mean?' I asked.

'I have to fill in the blanks on the reports we haven't written up.'

My fault again. I was the one in charge of writing up those reports.

'The handbook was instead of that,' I said.

'But the handbook didn't work out.'

'What handbook?' Alfie MacTalfie said.

'Would you like dinner, Mr MacTalfie?' I asked.

'Sure,' he said, forgetting instantly about the handbook. I took plates from the cupboard, and Dad took the chilli potatoes from the oven. He had prepared plenty in case Alfie stayed.

'I'll go to Inishnaroon solo,' I said. Just saying it made me wobble.

'We could both go next month,' Dad said.

'You'll have no locator by then.'

We all sat, and Alfie helped himself to three chilli potatoes.

'There's no point in you going solo,' Dad said. 'You're not allowed talk to humans.'

'Sure she is,' Alfie said. 'It's an Art Department assignment,' He spooned sour cream onto his second potato. 'Gotta get this recipe, Hal.'

'Why is an Art Department assignment different?'
Dad said.

'See, the Art Department don't update rules and
stuff,' Alfie said. 'Some rules haven't been seen for
decades. Centuries!'

In those olden days, he explained between
mouthfuls of chilli potato, human kids worked, and
so did fidder kids. Habits altered, and laws did too,
but the Art Department just ambled on. They didn't
actually hire kids any more, but the *rule* never

changed. Alfie told us he came across it a couple of months ago, when he was just nosing around.

'So you let fidder kids talk to humans?' I said.

'Technically, yeah. Until someone else finds the rule, and changes it. Right now it's legal.'

'Mr MacTalfie,' I said, 'I think your department is the tops.' Alfie MacTalfie scanned the table for more food. Dad pushed the fruit bowl towards him and Alfie looked scandalised.

'I better hit the road,' he said.

After Alfie left, Dad said, 'Inishnaroon seems very far away, Stevie. It scares me to think of you going there alone.' He was probably remembering Mom and Dicey and Annie vanishing. So was I.

'But like you say, Dad, some things we do, even if we're scared.' Saying that made me feel braver.

At last Dad said okay.

Now there was only one more thing I had to

ask him.

'Can I talk to Sandra May, Dad? Just one more time.'

Dad said I shouldn't talk to humans.

'But I'm working with the Art Department,' I said.

'Not with Sandra May, you're not.'

However.

Our 'Kids-Can't-Talk-to-Humans' rule was important, he said, but it wasn't our most important rule. Our most important rule was to Do Right By Our Human.

Doing right by Sandra May, he said, meant reassuring her that her imaginary twin sister wouldn't abandon her completely.

So, yes. I could talk to her, one last time.

It was late when I located to Sandra May's room. She was in bed, almost asleep, in those mismatched pyjamas. Her hair shone, and her eyes were soft. Her thoughts were meandering and sunny, and her mind was warm. What a change from when she first arrived in Tassimity.

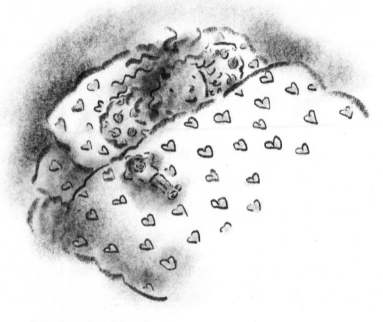

'Hi, Sandra May.'

'Stevie, hi!'

'I came to say goodbye,' I said. 'I'm going away.'

'Me too, Stevie! My Mam has a new job, and I'm going back to Linbradan soon.'

'Wow! That's amazing. Charlie though, he'll miss you.'

'I'll miss him too. But we'll visit each other. And guess what? He's friends with the Pink Frogs now, you know, Sean Cree's band? Charlie's writing songs for them!'

'Oh, I bet he's brilliant at that.'

'He sure is.' Sandra May paused. 'You know what, Stevie? You sound happier than before.'

She was right. My mind was sunnier too, now.

'I'll miss you, imaginary twin,' I said.

'I'll miss you too, Stevie. But when I think about you, no matter when or where, we'll kind of be together.'

I thought about it, and I saw she was right. And I knew I would often think about Sandra May Bee, and she would always be my imaginary twin sister, and my real, true friend.

Chapter 43

I stayed awake most of that night, making more changes to the handbook. I wanted it to be a book kids might like to read, fidder kids like my old school friends, or human kids like Sandra May and Charlie.

In the morning I keyed Mary Murphy's address into the locator. Dad and I held gaze, then I closed my eyes and pressed 'locate'.

The locator whirr accelerated to a dizzying spin.

whirr FIZZ

I opened my eyes.

Mary Murphy and her two dogs were sitting

outside their cottage, facing the wild Atlantic Ocean. She was wrapped in a hairy blanket and had a hat pulled over her ears, and she looked like she would never leave this seat, never mind write a book, even if I gave it to her word for word. One dog watched the gulls circling in the grey sky, the other lay on Mary Murphy's lap, shedding hair and snoozing. The air was tangy with salt and ozone.

I flitted onto Mary Murphy's shoulder and read the first sentence of my book.

'I remember seeing my first human like it happened just yesterday.'

She ignored me. Then a wind came up, and she hurried indoors.

'What if you only had a minute to help someone?' I said.

'That's a curious idea,' she thought. She took some paper from a drawer to write it down.

Darn it. I saw a stack of half-finished stories in

the drawer. Maybe Mary Murphy was not a finisher. I would need to stick to her like a magnet to get my book written.

So I kept pushing her, and she kept writing. She thought she was making everything up, as if she had invented the idea of fidders, and the departments, as if me and Dad didn't really exist. That suited me fine. I wanted our story written down, but I still wanted humans to think it was imaginary.

I kept her writing through the nights. I made

her cancel meeting her island friends. She wanted to write a book, so I told myself I was doing her a favour.

She tried to change some things, like making the Chief become sweet and kind, and Badger too. But I made her write everything down the way it really happened.

In a week, the whole book was written. Now Mary Murphy thought, 'It's not good enough to show anyone.'

Oh, please.

I went into full Minute Minder mode. 'Of course it's good enough! It's an amazing book!' I said. Then, trying to be honest, I said, 'Okay, maybe not amazing, but it's worth a shot, right? You did your best. What have you got to lose?'

So Mary Murphy sent the manuscript to her agent, and I went home to Dad.

It took a while, but that's how this book came to be published. Most likely you're a human reading this, not a fidder. Either way, you now know about being a Minute Minder.

If you're a fidder, you might actually want to become one. Minute Mindering is important work, and it's a good feeling, helping folks.

If you're a human, you can't help folks quite the way a fidder does. But you can do some Minute Minder work. You can give a minute to a human, or a dog or cat, or anyone who needs it.

You'll never be as good at Empathy Echo as I am. A human can't actually see exactly what another human is feeling or thinking.

But you almost can.

You can be kind. You can listen. You can make a difference. Isn't that what you want?

I feel sure, if you're still reading this book, that that is what you want.

Acknowledgements

I'd like to thank these good folks for their remarkable help.

Clare Pearson
my thoughtful, dynamic agent, for her commitment
and vision

Tommy, Anna, Mo, Maureen and Paddy
for lending me writing spaces while I was between homes

Nick, Patsy, Ed and Trish
for their generous, constructive feedback

Children's Books Ireland
for a whole week of writing in the Tyrone Guthrie Centre

The Pushkin Press team
especially Sarah Odedina, for her light, warm editorial touch,
and designer Jet Purdie, for his patience and mastery

The Arts Council of Ireland
for their terrific financial support, which allowed me
to write this book

AVAILABLE AND COMING SOON
FROM PUSHKIN CHILDREN'S BOOKS

We created Pushkin Children's Books to share tales from different languages and cultures with younger readers, and to open the door to the wide, colourful worlds these stories offer.

From picture books and adventure stories to fairy tales and classics, and from fifty-year-old bestsellers to current huge successes abroad, the books on the Pushkin Children's list reflect the very best stories from around the world, for our most discerning readers of all: children.

WHEN LIFE GIVES YOU MANGOES
IF YOU READ THIS
THE CASE OF THE LIGHTHOUSE INTRUDER
THE CASE OF THE HAUNTED WARDROBE

Kereen Getten

BOY 87
LOST
MELT
FAKE
WILD

Ele Fountain

THE MURDERER'S APE
SALLY JONES AND THE FALSE ROSE
THE LEGEND OF SALLY JONES

Jakob Wegelius

THE MISSING BARBEGAZZI
THE HUNGRY GHOST
INTO THE FAERIE HILL

H.S. Norup

HOW TO BE BRAVE
HOW TO BE TRUE

Daisy May Johnson

THE MYSTERY OF THE MISSING MUM
CITY OF HORSES

Frances Moloney

LAMPIE
GIRLS

Annet Schaap

SCHOOL FOR NOBODIES
THE THREE IMPOSSIBLES
THE DANGEROUS LIFE OF OPHELIA BOTTOM

Susie Bower

THE MYSTERY OF RASPBERRY HILL
THE MYSTERY OF HELMERSBRUK MANOR

Eva Frantz

LENNY'S BOOK OF EVERYTHING
DRAGON SKIN
THE WRATH OF THE WOOLINGTON WYRM

Karen Foxlee

THE TRUE ADVENTURES SERIES

BANDIT'S DAUGHTER
SWORDSWOMAN!
THE BLACK PIMPERNEL
THE FLAG NEVER TOUCHED THE GROUND
THE FOG OF WAR
THE GIRL WHO SAID NO TO THE NAZIS
THE MYSTERIOUS LIFE OF DR BARRY
QUEEN OF FREEDOM

SAVE THE STORY SERIES

THE STORY OF ANTIGONE: ALI SMITH
THE STORY OF GULLIVER: JONATHAN COE
THE STORY OF CAPTAIN NEMO: DAVE EGGERS

THE BLUE DOOR SERIES

THE SWISH OF THE CURTAIN
MADDY ALONE
GOLDEN PAVEMENTS
BLUE DOOR VENTURE
MADDY AGAIN

Pamela Brown

THE WILDWITCH SERIES

WILDFIRE
OBLIVION
LIFE STEALER
BLOODLING

Lene Kaaberbøl